PRAIS

"Holy shit! This book had me hypnotized. It's raw and rigorous and sexy and relentless and completely on fire — it's a cold beer beside an active volcano, and it's delicious. Like Chris Kraus and Maggie Nelson, *What Are You* wrestles critical theory to the ground and emerges with a triumphant, radical, thrilling, clarifying new form of writing about sex, feminism, and the self."

— KATE REED PETTY, AUTHOR OF *TRUE STORY*

"Lindsay Lerman is brilliant. This book manages to be fiercely direct and enigmatic at the same time. It hit me the way Duras, Zambreno, and Lispector do."

— NATE LIPPENS, AUTHOR OF *MY DEAD BOOK*

"An incantatory and hypnotic work of voice, *What Are You* exists at the apex of creation and destruction, desire and shame, innocence and experience, violence and tenderness, rapture and suffering, hunger and the denial of flesh. To read it is to feel the terror of falling from a great height—but wanting to; maybe even choosing to jump."

— SARAH GERARD, AUTHOR OF *BINARY STAR* AND *TRUE LOVE*

"*What Are You* is relentlessly and elegantly erudite, yet deeply felt and compulsively readable. There is nothing in literature, philosophy, or her own life that seems beyond Lerman's capable grasp. She has a particular genius for weaving together disparate elements that would leave a lesser writer dumbfounded."

— NICOLA MAYE GOLDBERG, AUTHOR OF
NOTHING CAN HURT YOU

"Lerman's prose evades categorical thinking and forces you to reconcile yourself to the fact that individuals and their worlds are dynamic, reflexive, and reciprocally determined. It's a slippery book that demands we deal with it in its full complexity, without recourse to the simplifying unities we would normally use to reduce people to what they aren't. Lindsay Lerman is insidiously powerful; you don't realize what she's done to you until it's done. Purgatory in the sense of catharsis, a text for devouring and devotion."

— CHARLENE ELSBY, AUTHOR OF *HEXIS* AND
PSYCHROS

"Lindsay Lerman gives a sense that the author and the reader are on the run together, foraging a path of discovery as they flee. With prose both beautiful and relentlessly shifting with experiment, this book meets the reader at not-knowing and carries them forward, scouting the territory just one step ahead."

— ALEX DIFRANCESCO, AUTHOR OF *ALL CITY*
AND *TRANSMUTATION*

WHAT ARE YOU

This is what I wanted to talk about.

LINDSAY LERMAN

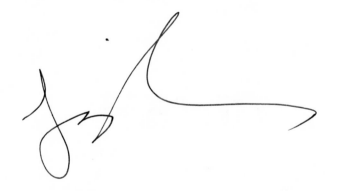

CLASH

CL◢SH

For the fools.

And especially for Tim and Aeyn, wherever you are.

"You stole me," Sophie said.

"I did not steal you very much," said the BFG, smiling gently. "After all, you is only a tiny little girl."

— ROALD DAHL, THE BFG

I propose a challenge, not a book.

— GEORGES BATAILLE, NOTES FOR INNER EXPERIENCE

PROLOGUE

The paradox of writing anything: I retreat into solitude in order to reach you. To reach *for* you.

The paradox deepens: reaching for you through the writing, there's too little of me left for those of you who don't need it, those of you I don't need to reach here, those who need the parts of me that do not exist here.

Where do I exist? And you—where are you?

Please know, reader, that I know just how many of you do not need me, and that I may need you most of all.

The pull of all these obligations—how do any of us handle them with grace?

I know that I am creatively bound by how I live, and that my living is bound by how and what I create. (Is it the same for you?) It may be a circular relationship, but it is not closed. What I have here is a fragile proposition—fragile like all living things —but its fragility does not mean it should be sheltered.

It is fine. I accept it.

————

I'm going, and I won't look back. Won't look back until I no longer need to see.

I just want to hold hands with you as we watch the world burn, knowing we burn next. Someone has got to go on believing. Let me be your fool.

———

What is this book? What is this thing? What do you hold in your hands? You hold the sound of someone living and dying, living and dying, trying to see. I don't know what it is. It's not up to me, anyway. None of this is an inventory, none of this is accusatory (or is it?), none of this adheres to a timeline, much as I wish it would. Watch as everything I thought I had understood recedes into the distance. Watch as I die. Watch as I am reanimated.

———

All people, places, and events depicted herein are both real and imagined, I'm sorry to say. "Like the church, like a cop, like a mother, you want me to be truthful,"[1] but Joni knew: then you turn it on me like a weapon. So you do not get to have it. It's not for you.

So I was wrong just a moment ago: I write not to reach you, but to reach through you, to what animates you. I am reaching past the person—through the person, all the way through—to the forces.

I understand that you'll be tempted to think of me as your narrator, but I don't recommend it.

I write to you as *no one in particular.* I need a new language. Please try to understand.

———

Hear the sound of my voice as I sing into the abyss, seducing it, drawing it near. Worry for me, dear reader. Worry for me, for you, for us.

PART 1

1

Dear You,

I have gathered evidence. In an attempt to understand you.

Evidence. (Noun: from late Latin *evidentia* for "proof;" the sense of "ground for belief" from late 14th century; "obvious," "apparent," "vivid presentation" from classical Latin; legal senses from c. 1500.) Whatever it is, I have gathered it.

Maybe I don't know what the evidence tells me—how or if it adds up to anything meaningful—but I do know that if I don't try to understand you, I won't make it.

Whatever you are, I need to know how to live in relation to you—there is no pretending you away—and I know that no one can survive you if they haven't earnestly worked to understand and anticipate you. I am in it for the long haul—I watch and I watch and I try to understand, every day. A lifetime of watching is long enough, wouldn't you say? Haven't I observed you enough? Haven't I seen everything in your smallest movements?

Place me at the scene: strung out, wrung out, nothing but sex and birth and growth and death and the push and pull between them. Like any organism.

———

I don't know how to live anymore. This is what you have taken from me. Or given to me, I guess, depending on how you look at it.

The other night, I was drunk, and I was sitting outside in the dark, watching the earth pulsate and glisten. I was sitting on the beach staring at the waves, the moon high above, and I was thinking of you. I was thinking of you.

I was remembering my 16th birthday, how I drank an entire bottle of coconut-flavored rum, how I hated myself for doing it. But there was no other way to stomach being so lonely and hungry and poor and tired, surrounded by terrible people I was supposed to call friends.

You were with me that night, though I didn't know it. You were starting to climb inside my dreams. You were coiling around my organs and my bones and my grey matter. You were already deep in my intestines, growing underneath my finger-nails. You were setting up shop in the back of me, watching me as I spoke, as I thought, as I loved. You were growing every day. Climbing in me, growing in me, reaching stretching gathering strength.

I had not wanted any beautiful boys or girls to kiss that night, but my friends had invited local college students, the guys from the aeronautical institute, thinking that's what I wanted, because it was what they wanted, or thought they wanted. I drank alone, and I was afraid. You were guiding me.

I was remembering that before I blacked out, I had taken a pen and my notebook outside, to write alone underneath the stars, but I was too drunk to write. When I went back inside and lost consciousness on the couch, I had two final thoughts: I hope no one rapes me, and I hope no one reads my notebook.

———

As I slept, you whispered to me, *One day you'll come apart baby—one day you'll come apart—and who will be there with you? Who will save you?* And in my dreams I blinked uncomprehendingly in response.

How do I know you whispered it to me? All I can say is that now I recognize the patterns. When you take form and press yourself further into me, this is your first threat and invitation.

The day after the party, I awoke, and all I could think was: *Don't go. I love you. I have no one to tell this to. Did you leave? Are you still here? Where are you?* Poor girl, I just didn't know.

2

"It is neither his person, nor the human personality in him, which is sacred to me. It is he. The whole of him. The arms, the eyes, the thoughts, everything. Not without infinite scruple would I touch anything of this." -Simone Weil, *Human Personality*

Back up. Back up, back so far up.

You. Can you hear me?

I have so much to say to you. Not just one of you but every You. So much to say I might never stop. I suppose it's been the work of my life, needing to say things to you, not knowing how. (The fear is gone for now. So I will see what I can say.)

I have written to each of you in secret, since the moment I could clutch a pen, marked each of you as You, as though I were afraid to write (speak) your name. You.

The yous who are friends, present and past. The yous who are lovers, ambiguous and clear-cut, long-lasting and one-night-only. The yous I never care to see again. The yous I might die to see again. The yous lost to pills and powders and ambitious death drives, the yous barely breathing but trudging on. The yous thriving, somewhere out there. Somewhere. The yous who forgot me long ago. The yous who I suspect will never forget me.

Oh to be strung out on your gaze—your reifying concretizing gaze. What the fuck am I going to do about it.

The yous who've put me to sleep and woken me up, drugged me and smacked me sober, brought me under, dragged me all the way down and then sent me flying, pushing me up up up. The yous who have cut me to the quick. Well, all of you have cut me to the quick.

Even you, the yous who groped me, poked me, held me down and threatened to rape and destroy me—yes, especially you. Each of you has shown me hell. That is, myself. You have shown me the conditions of my life, my existence.

I was tired of wanting to be you, knowing it wasn't possible. I smiled at most of you, accepted your desires as my own, addressed you only in secret. I slept on dirty floors for you, in parked cars for you, deep in the forest for you, to prove I was hardcore, I was cool, I had no needs, I could drink just as hard as you. I could handle it. I could handle almost anything. I made believe for you.

———

Eventually, everything you are catches up with you. Sometimes you're in your thirties, maybe your twenties. If you're lucky—or unlucky, I guess—it could be your forties, fifties. I was eight. Only eight. My tiny frame made tinier, and tinier. Was I crushed by the weight of it? Did I die in the wake of it? My best guess is yes. And yes and yes and yes.

Like Sylvia, I die with variety—have always died with variety.

You ask me what I know about obsession. If you only knew, you. If you only knew.

———

If you want me to tell you, to torture you, fine. Fine. I can pretend to be the site of your laundering, sure. But there's a "stake in your fat black heart"[1] and it's me. It was always me. Your fat fucking black heart. You forgot to guard it; you thought you didn't need it. You didn't know I could return from death—that I have always returned from death.

Some sad little bodies bear the burden of promising happiness more than others.[2] It's not an easy burden to bear, especially when you don't know that you're bearing it. Each of you has served as a reminder that while you were out there rushing headlong into *becoming yourselves*—becoming experts in science and seduction and social influence—I was just trying to survive. I was hiding from you or trying to outrun you or to find a way to give in without hating myself, knowing that with most of you, unless you set the terms, I would be in some kind of danger. But I want to bite the hand that feeds me. I want to bite it so fucking hard.

I keep walking to you with my arms extended, palms visible, possibility of threat erased, but it's time you saw how much of a threat this makes me. Has made me. I will no longer be the cheap thrill to distract you from the fact that your love is bullshit. It always has been. Again and again, again and again. The same shit, all these years.

Some of you know I am easily devastated. Some of you can see that I am nothing but an unhealed wound, vulnerable and foolish. And you can see that I know this but know no other way to exist, not yet. The smartest of you have understood how out of reach this makes me. Oh you want it all, do you? No you don't. I'm certain you don't.

I can tell you how each of you has nearly killed me as you

gripped my soul tight, but I'm not sure if I should. (How many of you had me wondering if you were going to kill me? How many times did I weigh *sex or death*? How many times could I not tell the difference? Did I like that?) I could also tell you that each of you has made me more alive than I have any right to be, despite you, because of you. Some of you are special. Many of you are not.

I saw the forces in you, but I could never figure out how to tell you. I saw them in each of your smallest movements, in your smiles and slow blinks and the way you bring food to your mouth.

The sun's going down slowly, like always, and I have nothing to lose.

This will be an exorcism, whether I want it to be or not. Through the person to the forces. To the forces. Nothing else matters.

———

Testimony: fragments, though they are already fraying.

Not without infinite scruple would I touch anything of this [3] indeed:

The you I met on the beach with friends, you who took my hand and said *Look at the bioluminescence*, and we watched the glowing waves pushing toward the shore and then receding. Such intimacy, the two of us watching the alien beauty together. You who explained your love of baseball in between pulls on the bottle of whiskey we were sharing, your blonde hair in your eyes. You who said you weren't used to girls who seemed smart.

The you who grabbed my skinny fourteen-year-old frame with the famished look in your eyes, your crazy burnout hippie eyes, open too wide, shifty but also somehow overly-focused. You who said *C'mere girl* from across the street, sing-shouting at me with such dazzling vagabond Charles Manson force that for weeks afterwards I felt sick to my stomach thinking of what could have happened had I listened to you, gone to you. I heard you say the words *warm wet parts*, and I ran. I ran and ran.

The you who said that loving me is walking into fire. You who said you were stupid enough to walk in anyway—to chase the fire, to chase love's slippery volatile certainty. You who have never really stopped writing to me, from the first clumsy puppylove poeticisms to the desperate and honest pleas for connection. You who know how words may be all we have to get through this life, the only worthless means, no end to the means in sight. You with your ability to derail, to bend, to edge closer to death.

The you I ended up kissing instead of hitting. I should have hit you, should have pushed you away with every bit of strength I could muster.

The you who has crossed that middle-age threshold and emerged full of death. You who twisted love into hate, seemingly overnight. You who send me death threats that ask *Why don't you love me.*

The you who said I'm only fucking your roommate to get to you. You who bought me all those drinks (I was only 18), danced with me all night, dismissed my innocent undergraduate stacks of philosophy books as self-help mumbo-jumbo, told me you loved my Middle Eastern features, ate the last jar of applesauce in my anemic fridge, dared your roommate to bare his cock in a boring attempt to shock and provoke me, to strip me of my innocence. (If you had only known, you. If you had only known how far off the mark you were.) You who shouted and pounded on the bedroom door when I locked it to keep you out, calling me a tease and a bitch and no fun. For months after, I hid in my apartment when I heard your front door above mine, opening and closing.

The you who performed "I've Just Seen a Face" at my request in a kitchen, at a party, everyone watching. You who did a fine job of embarrassing me during a performance in a big open park, shouting my name into the crowd, at a time when I was particularly intent on being invisible. You invited me shyly to lunch (you are still shy, for a performer, I think), and I was so clueless that it was days later when I finally understood the strangeness in your voice when I said I couldn't: it was something like disappointment, because it had been a date you were planning. I didn't know. I hadn't seen it until then. But you've hit the big time now, in big ways—I bet everyone else does the asking.

The you who punched through a window in Mexico when I had accidentally, unknowingly broken your heart. I had really been that oblivious. I had really been that self-centered. You had surprised me completely. I was that young. You were that young.

The you I could say almost nothing in front of. You who left me dumbstruck, silent in all ways but one. You who offered me something new with your additional silence—asking nothing of me, asking everything of me. You who reminded me that just existing alongside the right—or wrong—kind of person can detonate every single bomb in me. You with your need for control. Will you ever let go, I wonder.

The you who stole my number from our mutual friend, who called me day and night to say you'd leave your job, your apartment, your friends, for me. Me? But you don't know me, is all I could think. We spoke only once, is all I could think. You who said *All I want in this world is to sleep next to you.* But you don't know me, is all I could think. You who stopped calling when I said I'm falling in love with someone, and it is not you.

The first you, maybe—maybe the ür you—who holds the additional honor of being the first you ever to threaten sexual violence. (You were eight, I was seven.) You who wrote me letters to tell me you would sneak into my house at night and have sex with me while I slept. You who probably didn't even know the word *rape.* You who gave me my first taste of insomnia. You who scared me deeply enough to prompt me to ask for help from my parents, something I felt ashamed to do at the time, something dangerous in its own right. My insides still wince at even the thought of your name. For many years, my will to live would recede into the distance when I realized anew—each goddamn time—that you were the prototype. I am still trying to outrun you.

The you who had the audacity to force the deepest intimacy on a first date, rubbing my back tenderly as I threw up the sushi you'd insisted on paying for. It was clear right then to me that no amount of perfect mix CDs could crack my heart open for you, despite your charm and good looks and undeniable cool. You had said you were excited to date a cheerleader; I was not a cheerleader and never had been. You reached a greedy proprietary hand for the small of my back as we left the restaurant, and I could feel the desperate need to cry rising up within me. (*Is this all there is?* Yes. No. Sometimes yes, sometimes no.)

The you who wrote some of the first lines ever to split me open, to do that kind of loving damage good words can do. You with the intensity so great that even in my youth, I could see how your body couldn't contain it. You who cannot contain yourself. Do you see what a gift this makes you? What a gift you are to the animal kingdom, uncontained and fundamentally uncontainable? It is still an honor to be contaminated by you, to see you when I see you, to sit side by side with you.

The you who said that despite being gay, you were a tit man, and you dug my 70s tits. You were smarter than all of them—than everyone—you know. I remember the meals you made, each delicious one, how long your fingers were, how you drank your bourbon slowly, that you were the best at even the most difficult crossword puzzles, and that unlike the rest of us, you had the wisdom not to argue or to bash ideas against one another to understand and refine them, but instead to listen first and then respond thoughtfully, always with quiet dignity. I remember that time we snuck into the hotel pool out by the interstate, jumping the fence like the kids we didn't think we were. I remember when you visited us in Seattle and ate all the pâté we'd made for you, in record time. I remember the dream I had on the night you died. You were walking toward me on the sidewalk, a mixing bowl in your arm, a spoon in the opposite hand stirring the bowl's contents. *I'm here!* is what you said to me, as though you were just arriving, that smile taking up your whole face. I still cry helplessly, sad and alone and missing you, when I remember that dream and you. You.

The you who could not stop looking at me. You who appealed to my vanity with a gaze strong enough to make me think I was more than your (or anyone else's) reflecting pool. But god what a gaze. The kind of gaze that could—that *did*—stop anyone in its tracks, but right there, right in front of me, *for* me. (Life's camera is still operated by a man, I'm afraid. But I am trying to build my own camera.) I saw your façade crack once, and I loved you so much more for what I saw. We were at a bar watching a friend of a friend's band scream on a small smoky stage by the I-5—do you remember? A man wouldn't leave me alone, kept hovering and trying to whisper in my ear, circling me, over and over, and you stepped in to grab me, to suggest my takenness, and I saw a look of fear and helplessness wash over you. You hadn't meant to do it. You had meant to do it. I was taken, but not by you, and your face said that you were in danger of crossing a line you had only dreamed of crossing. I'm sure I'll never see you again.

You who put me up on the counter and took my entire mouth into yours. We couldn't stop smiling, couldn't stop thanking each other. We had it all, and we almost knew it.

The you who would stay up all night with me, drinking coffee and smoking cigarettes in Denny's, asking me what I wanted to do with my life, telling me college would be the best thing that ever happened to me. You gave me a hug that is still with me now—a hug that offered hope, despite its dangerous lingering quality. You couldn't have known at that time what a miracle it was for me to feel hope. Your back to the empty parking lot, you who said *You are special*, but all I could do was wonder why you didn't kiss me. You who spent a perfect summer day with me while your beautiful girlfriend was at work. It was the biggest my dreams got then—to be your other woman for a day. We wandered around town on foot, my shoulders a richer shade of red with each hour in the sun. We met compelling strangers and followed them to the Chinese restaurant, where we ate egg drop soup and imagined our futures anywhere other than *here*. All of us there, eyes locked across the table. You next to me, watching me. You who squeezed my hand tight, looked hard into my eyes, transmitting more than I knew how to receive. You who would later kiss me, for many hours and in many different places, even if it mattered little to me, because by then you were on your way out of my life. (How large was my appetite that even a lot was not nearly enough?) You who once took me by the hand and said *You might wanna be kinda high for this*, and there was no turning back. You who still haunt my dreams.

The you who only ever said *I don't like ambiguity—are you mine or not?* (Good luck with life is what I wanted to say.) You who said *There is something exotic about you, why are you hiding it from me?* You who said in every way possible *Show me who you are, show me show me*, with such force and precision that I couldn't get a word or a smile or anything in edgewise.

The you I needed to stay far, far away from. You who showed me just how much real desire—no matter how small—threatens the social order. What can be done? All I can say when I think of you is, what can be done?

The you above all yous, less a man than a pharaoh. The you who walked into class uncharacteristically late, on that sunny fall day, long hair in your face, broad swimmer's shoulders obvious, though you were not a swimmer. Someone said your name, said *Hi* and *Here's a seat*, and you took the seat as you smiled sheepishly but confidently. I looked at you and god help me all I could think was *There he is*. I couldn't help but love you. You who opened a portal. You who understand better than anyone I know that love most often manifests in ten thousand unsexy little sacrifices. The labor of love. Because we love each other enough to know that love is not enough, once the infatuation drugs are gone, and that without the labor, the unsexy labor, the love itself —on its own—doesn't stand a chance. You with a power that comes from the untouchable core of you.

———

I have known what there is to see in each of you. I have known what is not there to see. I have never known what to do about it.

The best of you have reminded me that I cannot confuse scraps for meals. That it is not easy to be me, and that I can't go around shaving off whole parts of me, swallowing entire dimensions of me in order to believe the story—the boring lie—that I have simple and uncomplicated desires or that I'm not drawn to danger and pain as a means of testing and strengthening and understanding myself. With you, I remember that I have no business thinking that I move through the world with ease. What a boring, thoughtless thing to have tried to tell myself anyway. I need more. Have needed more. More and more and more. If Simone Weil is right that personality only emerges with error, then oh god you have all seen me. Seen me and seen me and seen me, no matter how much I tried to hide.

The worst of you. What can I say? Who you are is no longer the question. Only why. Why why why. I leave you here. I have never wanted your little control games—I have wanted someone to jump off the cliff with me, and now I can finally say it. All these years you have asked me if I'm ready to suffer—winking at me, like *Toughen up, baby*—but I don't believe you ever understood what you were asking.

I don't know how to live without you, but I have to. Living with you is killing me. It's killing everything in me.

I need to stop being killed. No more outrage for you. Beyond outrage is an honest reckoning with myself. It's my business what happens there, in that place. Not yours, even if you are still with me.

If I've lost my liquid nature, I need to find my way back.

3

You approach me like the night approaches the window. Except no, that's not quite right, because it always seems like you're already here. Still, somehow it feels like the way the night sneaks up to the window.

———

You told me about the Zen master you had gone to see. You wondered if I wanted to come with you to see him. You said it's important to learn how to let it all wash away. Sounds good, I thought.

The Zen master said to watch it all appear and then to watch it fade and dissolve and to withhold judgment. And I wanted to listen so closely, I wanted to really hear him, but he was looking down my shirt, and I felt afraid. He said *Come closer* before I left, but I could not. *Open, open,* he said, *the way you open all your holes to someone in the night,* he said. Open, open, but I would not.

I saw you watching. I saw.

I saw that you need a game to play, otherwise you get bored and start to kill.

I wasn't sure, though, that I had really seen it. Maybe my eyesight was bad. Maybe it still is.

4

D o you remember the time I told you that you had broken my heart? Do you remember that I said you had taken poor care of my soul, flicking it away after begging for it?

How I wanted you to want my love. At the time, I thought I saw clearly that your problem was that you couldn't give or receive anything, but I am no longer sure of such assessments. I hear through the grapevine every single year that you want to kill yourself.

You were a god to me once.

I don't care if you're suicidal. If you want to do it, I know I can't stop you. I don't care if you're done living. You want to disappear down in Colombia, you find reason to tell me again and again, night after night, alone on your mountain. *So alone, so alone,* you say—you're so so alone. I wonder if you remember that I once loved you, you and only you, with all the force of me, and you threw me away.

You are the logical conclusion of you.

———

Do you remember the night I gave it to you—the thing you had wanted? You had your guitar. I had my voice. We had songs. But we had no other instruments of communication. We sat there for hours, in a dark and empty room, singing our bodies to each other, knowing no other way to reach each other, wishing we could be more than we were. I miss singing with you. I miss watching you.

I don't care if you don't remember. But I know you do. No one had yet asked you to show them you. I was asking you with everything in me to show me you.

Do you remember the letter? It was an email, in fact, that I printed on paper and folded into a neat square. For years, I kept it with me everywhere I went, such was the intensity of my silent obsession. Even now, I know I may never receive such a *letter* again. What did it say? It said that you had found me inside you somehow, and that you were surprised, afraid. You hadn't expected to find me there. I was not in your plans.

———

You could do it all, you know—you *were* all, everything, every last thing. You were a god with your guitar. No one could not be transfixed when you opened your mouth, employed your gaze.

I would watch you create—your voice from another world, your arms wrapping nearly all the way around the guitar and back (what would I be like in your arms, I wondered, would I be different)—and I saw so much beauty—so unpossessable, so sovereign—it frightened me.

Was I a child? I don't know. But I would blink in wonder— was I your proud possession, were you singing for me, was I your muse, oh please say yes—and in the midst of my wonder, I was gripped by a coiling, swirling fear that I would never know beauty like it again. Maybe only you could show me.

Like any other addict, I clung to you for the narcotizing, paralyzing effects of the beautiful things I thought only you could show me. I believed every word, listened as your perfect voice wiped every slate in me clean. But tiny baby me, I had no knowledge of just how intertwined creation and destruction are. I did not yet know that someone with as much creative force as you is also necessarily—if sometimes accidentally—destructive. Creator, you destroyed me.

(How I wanted your destruction.)

———

The truth is that I destroyed you right back with my quiet honesty, the only tool I had at my disposal, though destroying you was not my intention. I did not know why—and still do not know why—I bothered to say it, but I did. I said it. *You hurt me.*

Three small words, and it all came undone.

You shed a real tear—it rolled right down that magnificent sculpted-marble cheek before you had time to hide it. Do you remember that you told me, as we parted ways that night, that you'd never known anyone so alive? What a graceful goodbye. Fuck you for that.

Do you remember? *I have never known someone so alive,* you said, looking at me.

I had stood my ground, as I had coached myself to. I stood strong and tall, but really I was on my knees. On my knees begging *Love me like I know you can, and I promise I'll never ask for anything again.*

But we had nothing left to show each other, and I see now that you did not have that love to give—it could not be given. We were over, whatever we were, and though I knew I was supposed to be proud, I just felt sad. I was alone with my worthless dignity. Worthless adult dignity.

———

And now you want to die.

Does it follow you every day, the desire to give in to your great destructive power? Have you been able to show yourself to anyone, ever? Is it all destruction with you now, or is there still some creation? You say you're up there on the mountain, like some bastard god with dwindling insight, drinking to pass the time. Again I don't blame you. But how can it be that, as far as you're concerned, no one needs you? All these years—twenty of them, at this point—we have been striving to understand each other, to see each other, to *communicate*, and you can't see the significance of that?

The question I have to keep asking, I'm not sorry I will not stop: how to give everything—a hunger-satisfying kind of giving —but only to those who know what to do with *everything*, to those who are not afraid of their own giving? We can think we know how to tell the obliged, the gratified, from the thankless, but sometimes we just need to be received. And we lie to ourselves. I see now that giving can be a way to refuse receiving. Why has it taken me so long to understand that what any of us cannot give is also what we cannot accept?

And the fact is that the memory of my giving, of my desire to create with you, has haunted you in ways that have been more destructive to you than I ever could have imagined. It took time, but I believe I did just as much creating-destroying as you, without even knowing it.

Why else do you call out to me, lonely god needing his playthings.

5

Whatever you are, I know that you once were afraid to touch me, but that stopped. You stopped being afraid to touch me, and that's where all the trouble began. I do not like how much I liked the trouble.

Should I keep singing to you, hoping you can hear?

6

Tonight I'm in seventh grade, when I won the school-wide spelling bee. The entire middle school is watching. You and your friends and *you* are watching. I wonder if you remember.

I must have beamed with pride as I confidently spelled the final word. It was *salmon*. The only other remaining contestant had left out the *l*. It seemed like a lucky break; there were plenty of other words I didn't know how to spell.

When it was all over, and we were shuffled back to our classrooms, our teacher, Mrs. ____ reached into her desk and pulled out a Kit Kat for me. In front of everyone, she told me she was proud of me.

Later in the day, after lunch, you approached me, to show me something on your hand. You had taken a red marker and drawn blood on your middle finger, dripping onto the back of your hand. You said it was from finger-banging me, because I had my period.

You showed your hand to your friend standing next to you, and you both laughed. You laughed hard, and with complete confidence. The two of you shared a conclusive, triumphant look, and you walked to the other side of the classroom. I didn't have my period then—hadn't had it even once yet—but that's beside the point.

Mrs. _____ overheard the exchange. She said nothing. As far as I know, she never said anything to you.

I didn't say anything either. My face turned red, and I fought back tears for the rest of the day.

―――――

In fact, no one had to say anything, to anyone. Order had been restored. I was terrified and humiliated. You were in charge and intimidating. You wrenched back all the power you were sure you deserved—that you knew how to possess, even as a child.

You were not the straw that broke the camel's back, but you could have been close. You were a particularly heavy straw— such a heavy straw—because you didn't just go after my body, like the rest of them. You were the very first to also go after my intellect, so skillfully, so quickly. I understood that the rest of my life would be negotiating you. All five thousand million billion of you.

There is only one reason why I did not kill myself in the wake of the knowledge: there was something I liked about how you showed me to myself. It made me electric and lonely.

―――――

No, stop. Throw this letter away. I'm not happy with it. This is not how I want it to go.

This isn't what I wanted, this isn't quite right. This is not reaching beyond the person to the forces. This is not breaking up with the universe. This is not what I wanted.

Keep going.

7

The next time, it was dark, so dark, pitch black everywhere, and you swept in so fast, I couldn't make out what was happening, but I could see what the night had done to you. I saw something new. I saw that you only lived there, in the night—that it was the only place you could live, but that you also didn't *really* know how to live there, or maybe anywhere. I saw that you could only succumb to it, never stand up to it.

I saw that the night tore you apart and had you convinced that you could not withstand anything real, real like looking at yourself being pulled apart, spilling open, dissolving, tearing. I saw what the night had done to you. I couldn't see anything else, but I could see this.

You did not understand that the night is to be resisted sometimes. But how? How could you not understand. I was just a child, you were not. How could you not see? Maybe you *were* the night—maybe that's why.

And what was wrong with *me*? I could learn how to hold the night off, but not how to hold you off. You were still growing steadily within me. How?

———

Something can shake up your entire sensorium—throw every way of knowing, feeling, perceiving into crisis—and that is called trauma, but what if each constitutive block of the sensorium is wrong, so wrong, and there isn't *shaking up* so much as *continually permeating bad*? How do you get it out?

———

It stayed dark the whole time. You were sweeping through me and through me, wringing me out. I was a piece of broken glass tumbling in the surf. I was being inhaled and exhaled by something. Something. It was dark. It stayed dark.

I was so scared for you to see me naked.

Soon it was over, and you said *See you in the next world, baby*, and I stood silent and motionless—incapable, as always. Everything spilling out of me.

8

I was in my late twenties, and then my early thirties, when I began to realize that I was meeting you. I had always been meeting you, I just hadn't known it.

You tore straight into me. You were impervious, imperious—the embodiment of literature, of art, of serious thought, of intellectualism. You were beautiful and in full possession of yourself. You were never alone out in the desert like Chris Kraus's Dick, but you did such a good job of playing the loner rebel cowboy, always. (Loner rebel cowboy ethic: life is for me. Making visible to me my pathetic shtetl ethic: life is with people.)[1] Most of your vassals (vessels) didn't have the capacity to distinguish between the real thing and the simulacrum anyhow. It's why you had your power to begin with.

Would you believe that by the first time I really met one of you, at maybe 26 years old, I was already worn out by living? Does it sound melodramatic to you? *Weak?* Well, it's true. Living as I was *supposed to* had begun to break me. I wonder if you know what I'm talking about.

I like a challenge. So I wanted to show you things. (You who might not have been capable of sight; I do see my stupidity.)

You were so much worse than Chris Kraus's Dick. You were

real, but you were unnameable, maybe even ineffable. And you were everywhere. Everywhere everywhere. It was like once I saw you, you blossomed and spread, enjoying being seen.

I know that's not how it works, but that's how it felt. You were just like the Zen master looking down my shirt.

———

It helps to try to give you a name. Names, even.

Dear _____, Why did I know all this and still feel so hunted, so devoured by you? Because although you are just squatting, you have a vast system—a vast *system of systems*—in place to protect you where you are, as you are. Imperious. Impervious. That one little 'v' multiplies your power into perpetuity.

Dear _____, Why have you never used your power to do anything interesting? You know you could take any chance you like, and it would be celebrated. Forfucksake, "TEACH ME A NEW LANGUAGE, DIMWIT."[2]

Dear _____, Why have I always known all this and still resigned myself to conflating hunting, and being hunted, with your love, with your respect, with *the real thing*?

The clarity of heartbreak, _____—I've got it on my side. The clarity of heartbreak. It's a kind of sobriety, something like coming up to the surface. I wonder if you've ever felt it, if you've ever needed it. You were never going to love me, _____. You don't love, you don't think, you don't create. You take possession. Now I understand. (It's the same grift with all of you, everywhere.)

Dear _____, I wonder now—I think I'll never stop wondering—why you've always needed to reduce my existence to a series of unfortunate personal problems. Because none of it is accidental; so very little of it is personal. You've got your grift down—I can't stop seeing it.

Dear _____, I wish I could make you see: I have no interest in pulling heartstrings for the sake of pulling heartstrings. What is the *content* of this heartbreak, these little personal problems?

What can be *done* with our forms of heartbreak? Each time you've scoffed at me for feeling, for having those pathetic things called feelings, I have seen just how weak you are.

Dear ____, I see that every time you have asked me to cross some distance between us, you have turned that distance into quicksand. And every time I have tried, and I have sunk, deeper and deeper, choking on you, drowning in you, accepting my death, accepting it as my own fucking fault. But.

But but

But dear ____, there has always been a cost to having me. One day you'll see it. The bill collectors will come after you. I have always known that there's a cost to being had. I have never been able to not pay.

Dear ____, Will I be punished for saying this? How permanent will you make my exile? I don't care anymore.

It's worth the risk, ____. It was always worth the risk.

9

Fine. Here it is.

 I'm silent, looking at you in my memory now, but behind the silence, I am shouting. Shouting: *fine*. Here's the one I don't want to remember.

You took a form. The division began to break down.

———

It was not a dream, but no one would have believed me if I had told them. It was a series of waking dreams. I kept them to myself.

You put me in your car, your eyebrows raised in challenge. You rolled a cigarette and looked straight at me. I raised my eyebrows back and told you to open a beer.

We drove all day with the windows down, going nowhere in particular, the heat pouring in. We stopped only for beer and cigarettes and looking at views. I spilled a half-drunk can on my shirt and pulled it off at the stoplight, without apprehension. Everything necessary seems deeply *un*necessary, when so much trouble is on offer.

We pulled off at the lookout near the small destitute former mining town—the one tumbling slowly down the mountain—taking in the enormity of the view—the endless layers of dirt and rock and their jagged edges and the sky with its smears of clouds. We opened another beer to share, your arms around my bare waist as I leaned back into you to see better, farther. Do you remember?

Later that night, around a bonfire your friends had built, you tried to take pictures of me, but I hid my face. I'm not sure why. Your gorgeous mystic friend, Crystal or Amber or Jade—the one I could tell you'd had lots of sex with—took me by the hand and said in her floating voice *Beautiful girl, he wants your picture to remember all of you. You'll be one of his queens.*

Please don't make me say it. Fine, I'll say it. I had never been so happy to be someone's prey. I had spent days and nights and days and nights nurturing my obsession, silently asking the universe to encourage you to stalk me, and here we were—in a fantasy come to life—and I was denying you my face for your memories. I wouldn't give you *all of me.*

What would you have done with all of me?

Now I see (do I?): you were the beginning of my understanding that getting what you want usually offers less meaning than the wanting itself and the aftermath of the getting. Being flooded with such knowledge is always overwhelming. Hiding in the face of it is not wrong. Thank god I knew to hide, to disguise what was worth protecting.

Gorgeous Crystal/Amber/Jade braided my hair and massaged my shoulders, showing me the tattoos around her ankles, describing all the men who'd given her the rings and bracelets she wore, telling me I should consider getting a little high with her. She said she would read my cards someday, when I was ready.

Your poet friend said he had some notebooks in the car he needed to burn with you, and together—solemnly, as though it were some ancient ceremony—the two of you retrieved his notebooks and slowly tore out page after page, dropping them into the fire and smiling at each other as they burned.

I had never seen such life. Such *living*. It was as though I'd found my way into an alternate universe. I wanted to find a body of water—I thought it would help me understand. Let me swim, and I can find a way to understand. Please let me swim. But we were landlocked, no water for miles and miles.

I asked you if it was getting close to midnight, knowing it was well past midnight, when I was supposed to be home, and you kissed me and said *Yeah I think it's a little later than that,* some laughter in your voice. I felt my naïveté and my inexperience anew, both of them swelling up in me like the feeling of needing to cry.

I could feel your poet friend's eyes on me. I felt his desire aimed at me. Holding my gaze, you nodded in his direction, as though you understood something. You were teaching me how to cast spells. I saw how to stop time. How to bend it and stretch it.

You were giving me permission to be anything I wanted.

————

I should not have needed your permission.

Months earlier, you had unlocked me with a single sideways glance. You had been giving me such permission to live ever since. There is still nothing sexier.

It has happened since then, but there is no doubt that you had more to teach than most. Do you see why it happened? Do you see? I should not have needed it; it should not have been sexy. Do you see? It was all wrong.

Your neighbor showed up with the weed, and everyone cheered. I napped in the dirt, willing away the knowledge that it was 2:00am, and people might be worried about where I was, when I'd come home. Compared to all this, home offered nothing—less than nothing. Home was a great chasm I would fall into the moment I crossed the threshold, and the fall would knock out most of my newfound knowledge of living.

So I would stay as late and as long as I could, hoping to build something strong enough to withstand the fall and its damage. Why could I not see, until now, that it was me who was doing the building?

You woke me up gently, taking me by the hand, wrapping me in a blanket. We watched the stars on the hood of your car. I felt the pull of exhaustion. Someone threw a bottle into the dying fire. You unwrapped me and said *There's so little meat on you*, as if I were your next meal. You touched my neck, and I may as well have been dead.

I want to capture the texture of that feeling—the pain and the possibility and all the giving in and submitting and pushing back, pushing away as you surged through me—but I can't. Maybe I *was* dead.

Do you remember?

Where are you now? Are you living in your aging parents' basements? Are you dead? Why are there so many of you?

10

I feel you advancing sometimes, and I have to admit, there's some pleasure in the dread. I'm a live wire when you come around.

———

I have the feeling that if I could get you in a room and sit you down and get you all the way still, I could look into you and see —and I think I know what I would see, but I keep coming up against the fact that you can't be located. I don't know what you are, let alone where you are.

I only know when I can feel you in me. And I don't even know that I know it; I can only feel it.

———

I did too many drugs trying to find you, to feel my way to your location. Out in the forest, too stoned, thinking about the forms you take, and I'm lost—the fungus, the mold, the insects, the people. The people? (Me?) The rain? The clouds? The earth? The grocery store? The lobsters scrambling in the tank? Vivaldi playing on the radio?

Some of your forms are just an endless loop of exploitation, but some of them are not. Do they achieve symbiosis? Why can I not understand?

It remains unclear why which are which, and how. I don't know why I'm thinking this, and I don't know what it helps me to understand. The strangest thing is that I think I might understand you. I'm beginning to suspect that you've spent more time in me than I know.

I run my hands through the moss and over the bark and over the cotton of this shirt and through my own hair, and I wonder if you can feel it too, feel it through me, as me. When I touch my face, is it you?

———

I think I know what you want—to consume my flesh, take it into you, and become some new kind of corporeality through the consumption of me, but I want to tell you that I don't think it's possible. Not with me, anyway.

PART 2

11

It doesn't let up—you don't let up. Why do you keep coming back for more? Or is it me—am I the one coming back.

It's always time to write when I dream of you fucking me. Put me under, put me under. I want it to feel like swimming.

In the dreams, you nod in the direction of the living room floor—at least that's what I think it is, nodding, a floor—and it's over before it's even begun. My body is yours to beat. Sometimes it does feel like swimming.

But when I wake up, I see that it happened; it was both dream and not. I never understand. You never play fair.

———

And I wonder what's wrong with me, because I kept thinking that if I held perfectly still it would all dissolve, you would wash away, slide right out of me. But no. You keep reappearing, no matter how still I stand.

One time, there were confused tears streaming down your face (is it a face you have?) as you approached me, and I wondered if you were scared or sad. Is it possible? Was it love?

Did I watch you collapse under the weight of whatever you are?

Is it possible?

———

I fit right into you, you keep reminding me, and you fit right into me, too.

I fit into you, and you fit into me, and maybe it was and is even more hell. You were incomplete without me, you'd say. Each time. Each and every time. You begged me to fuck you on the living room floor. You begged and begged, and I felt a sinking doom. A spreading doom. A surging doom, like something was inescapable. Like as long as I could breathe, it would stalk me. Was *it* you?

Either way, I was stupid enough to be flattered.

But there is no more living room floor to fuck on. No living room and no floor. No nothing.

I don't even think there is time—there isn't even the thing called *time* in which it might occur. How is any of it possible?

I think I glimpsed once that your secret is that you are very quiet mostly, and only occasionally loud. It's not what we're used to. We make so much noise. But you, you don't feel the pressure to make a point when there isn't one to make. Your cruelty—if that's what it is—is the quiet kind.

12

You took my face in your hands, and I was no longer sure of what existed and what did not. That's how bad it was. You reached for me, and your body said, *Are you ready to suffer?*

At that point, I had been burning for so long that I didn't know what was left of me. Had I released too many pieces of me? Overextended my insides? Or maybe I had burned too hard and too fast, been reduced to a pile of ashes.

At that point, I dreamed of you all the time. Way too often. I must have known it was trouble once you started invading my sleep.

———

You carry me with your gaze. You make me real, allow me to dissolve, to disappear. They always say this is the danger. So now I know.

Even still, you make me real. Even still, I want your eyes on me.

———

I've taken Tony Hoagland's assessment of D.H. Lawrence seriously, and I can say I've begun to see what he meant when he called Lawrence, "a man who burned like an acetylene torch from one end to the other of his life,"[1] and I see that we don't understand burning. We've allowed it to be romanticized. We've been sold a false bill of goods. We don't see its power to change real, actual lives—to fuck it all up. I see it now. We've fetishized it. We do not know what to do with the real thing.

Burning is a gamble. And those who do it are the kind of powerful people for whom the deepest darkness is a distinct possibility—a result of the gamble. I have seen it happen. Sometimes the only thing people can think to do with their freedom is to oppress, enslave, snuff out.

And I am tired of reading all your radical takes on living as a self without a Self, on becoming a body without organs, on stretching capacities into the realm of impossibility, psychic nomadism—all of it. It has become a boring masturbatory show of *thinking about burning.* You want desire to challenge the social order, but you never let it do that. You never ever do.

I no longer trust your thinking about burning, especially if it glosses over or ignores the possibility of that particular darkness that accompanies the burning—that darkness that has to be resisted, lived alongside in constant tension. It's all just a trend to you, something to try on and purchase and eventually discard. Or you want to have a weekend with it, bingeing and bingeing until you've had your fill. I cannot, will not trust it. Not after having begun to burn. Not after having lived while on fire.

It's just a sexy way of adapting to the impossible demands of late capitalism or whatever the fuck we're barely living through —a defensive tactical decision dressed up as ontology—because it has required a constant upgrading, remaking, and forgetting of ourselves, moving with it where it tells us to go, doing what it tells us to do, in order to survive.

But burning is different. It is not an adaptive strategy. Maybe we've conflated some things that ought to remain distinct.

I don't think you've understood any of the demands you issue. I don't think you have any idea what you mean when you ask me if I'm ready to suffer. I don't think you have any idea what it means to dissolve into nonself. Nonself unself ir-self a-self whatever, I don't think you understand.

How did I get here? I don't think I like it here. I think I want off this ride.

————

Stop falling in love with me. It's nothing but a distraction. I'm tired of being your distraction. Your love does not burn. It's all wrong. I know I keep saying that, and I know I seem crazier with each utterance, but it's true. It's all wrong. Keep your love away from me—far, far away from me. Your heart is nowhere near the love you offer. It's like your heart has left your body.

Why are you here? (By which I mean, why am I here.)

Keats says that there's a holiness to the heart's affections, and I have never found cause to disagree, no matter how badly I wanted to, no matter how many times the world has laughed at this reluctant certainty. This is the difference between burning and distraction. We don't get to *not burn*. We have to pay for this consciousness, this bodilyness, this neediness, this vulnerability. We can defer payment for as long as we can manage, but there will be late fees. Or the collection agencies will come after us. There's no way out. If we give all the way into it, we're done. If we refuse to see it—pretend it's not real—we're also done.

But I am trying to refuse to understand it as condemnation. It is holiness. It is complicated, like all gifts.

————

I have wanted you to tell me that you love me, but by the time you can say it, I know you well enough to know that you cannot mean it. It's not possible; you cannot mean it. If you haven't

burned and understood the possible outcomes and then begun
to work very hard in the direction of the liberating ones, you just
can't mean it.

I have loved you, each time, until you've shown me how
not to.

───────

How has it ever been real? I don't know, but when it has been
real, there has been burning. I've died in each fire.

If we have ever burned together, you've shown me everything you refused to show me. I almost wish it weren't the case;
it's not easy to see others burn. Your pride falls away. Your
posturing disappears. You are not clever, not smart. You are ugly,
and so you become beautiful. I can see a breeze blowing right
through the very core of you. Of me. When you offer your mouth,
you offer the apocalypse. "There is a murder that assassinates
us, it's not you, it's not me, but between you and me, between
my love and your love there is murder."[2]

───────

I am selling myself to you. What's my price? (Everyone wants to
have one.)

This. You.

I pay myself with you; I am the one swindling myself. You
will forget me, but I will still be here with this burning. I will still
be here, fire running all through me. You will forget me, but I will
still be here. I will still be here, watching as you drive away,
leaving me to burn alone, you refusing to feel everything I have
no choice but to feel.

───────

Long after you've forgotten me, I will remember the sound of you, the taste of you, the weight of you, and I will remember it all as feeling. Long after you've forgotten me.

I am powerless in front of you, naked as I've ever been. Powerless and naked, crawling on my hands and knees. You walked in on me living my life, and I was exposed. So exposed, I may as well have been stepping out of the shower under the gaze of an intruder. I understand that my willingness to be here makes me more powerful than I can yet know.

———

It's only when my face is in your eyes—when I am carried by your gaze—that I understand how essential the burning is. (Why? Why does it have to be this way?)

The rest of the time, I'm just trying to get by. Up all night, living it through thinking it, wondering if my organs will melt and dissolve inside me, I feel just how alone I might be. It's when I wonder if I'm dying that I might be most alive. *This is what it is to want.* I'm just trying to get by.

To want is to be uncontained, uncontainable. To want is not to have a need—it is to be desire itself. It is to exceed yourself. It is so much work.

And I don't know if it's worth it.

13

Sometimes you need me to see that you do not love me. I see it, and I accept it. I accept defeat, like I always have. You do not love me—fine—so why be in me?

Why do you come around like a cat, saying, *Just so you know, I don't love you, and you're not really real, and neither are your attempts at understanding.*

———

At some point, I started learning from you. Somewhere along the way. Each time I moved to a new school, a new house, a new life, I found the queen bee, and I took her down rapidly, in full view of everyone else, knowing there was no other way to make it. It was not what I wanted—none of it was what I wanted.

It was moving in the wrong direction. All flows moving in the wrong direction. I need to reverse, move them back toward you.

———

Are you gone? Maybe you are.

I think I like my life better without you. Still, there is empti-ness where you were. I am still afraid that I will die if I cut you out. Afraid that I will die, as if you were Heathcliff. As if I were you. It's like you're here but not.

You leave a trail of misery like little glowing pebbles in the moonlight, like crumbs in the forest, because you can see that I want the terrifying solitude of a thick grove of trees, and I follow you to my own continual death. You kill me again and again, not seeming to notice that each time you hold me, you are holding a dead woman.

14

Did you know that shortly after Rainer Maria Rilke and Lou Andreas-Salomé met, he *changed his name on her recommendation*? René to Rainer, just like that.

Do you know anything else about Lou Salomé? That Nietzsche fell for her like a schoolboy? Yes, Nietzsche.

I wanted to tell you. I wanted to find you, to call you, to write you a letter, to email you, to find you, to tell you.

I know that I must keep leaving and leaving, but still.

———

Yes, Nietzsche. The story goes that he wanted total possession of her, and she refused him.

What advice does the old woman offer Zarathustra when he complains about women, asserting that they can be explained away by the possibility of pregnancy—by the very fact that they are reducible to their reproductive capacities? "You go to women? Do not forget the whip."[1]

Have you read much, I wanted to ask you, about how she had a celibate marriage to Friedrich Carl Andreas, while she was also married to Paul Rée?

I wish you could write a history of me, of you, maybe of me and you.

———

This is what I wanted to talk about.

I knew you, or thought I was beginning to know you, so I knew that maybe you knew that Salomé's relationship with Freud is the most well-documented—Freud being Freud. And I knew that you might know that Freud once claimed that before Salomé, he had "never before met with such a deep and subtle understanding of analysis."[2]

Do you know that Salomé consistently challenged Freud on the patriarchal underpinnings of psychoanalysis, on his thin "ideas on female libido,"[3] and on desire's shameful and dark connotations in psychoanalysis—connotations that lead, in psychoanalysis, to the need for repression? Do you?

———

I am angry that little more than her correspondence with a famous man has been translated, and I know that you are responsible for this. It's your fault.

The problem is that all is forgiven when I look into your eyes. (Eyes? Face? Again I don't know what you have, what you are.)

I have wanted to write similar words to you, but I knew they would fall on deaf ears: "If for years I was your woman, it was because you were for me the first real truth—undeniable proof of life itself. Word for word, I could have repeated to you what you said to me as a confession of love: 'You alone are real to me.' With these words we were wed, before we had even become friends... Two halves did not seek completion in each other. But a surprised whole recognized itself in an unfathomable totality."[4]

It's so simple. It's so impossible.

———

The first known Salome—the Biblical one—demanded and received the head of John the Baptist. On a platter. She exists as a cautionary tale (for all of us?).

Lou Salomé: "Rooted since the beginning in the substrate of all existence, eroticism grows from a soil that is ever the same, rich and strong, to whatever height it grows, whatever the immensity, the space occupied by the marvelous tree in which it flowers—subsisting—even when that soil is entirely overrun by edifices—below them, in all its primeval, obscure, and earthy strength. [...] Thus we find eroticism associated with the almost purely vegetative functions of our physical being, bound closely to them, and even if it does not become, like these functions, an absolute necessity of existence, it continues to exert a powerful influence upon them. That is why, even in its elevated forms and manifestations, even at the topmost point of the most complex ecstasies of love, there remains in it something of the simplicity and profundity of its origins, always present and ineradicable—something of that healthy gaiety which experiences the life of the body—in the specific sense of the satisfaction of the instincts—as always new, always young and, so to speak, like life itself in its primitive sense."[5]

Do you see why I wanted to write to you about her? Do you see why I think I'm dealing with something that might exceed the order of knowledge?

Do you see why I found Bataille—someone who understood that whatever eroticism is, it's a kind of haunting? Someone who understood the haunting, the forces. Someone who must have known you.

I am desperate for the ones who must have known you. I look for them everywhere, every day, once I know that looking is a possibility for me. I cannot stop trying to find them, because each time I do find one of them, I see that I might not be crazy. At least, not crazy in the ways I've been told to understand crazy.

———

Eroticism is not the point, though.

Or maybe it is. Because it exceeds sexuality-individuality-humanity, it is stuffed into odd-shaped, shifting, inadequate categories, but because it exceeds, it keeps resisting all these attempts at capture, at mastery. It keeps pushing out of every frame of reference. It is the movement of the ocean meeting the land, the push and pull, the hissing, the begging, the retreat and return. It eludes even you—I have seen it. You laugh the loudest laugh when I bring this up to you.

But I know that I have seen something, and I have to learn to trust it. If I am made of the stuff that exceeds, why are you in me, why are you going to all this trouble to be in me, and what am I doing, when I make my tiny self domesticated and digestible, assisting you as you keep doing it to me, for me?

Do you hear me?

15

I said *All the way through,* didn't I?

   I said it, and I meant it: the closer we got (by which I mean, the more I felt you in me), the lonelier I became.

Why didn't I see this as a problem? Why haven't you told me to stop?

   All the way through: what are you?

16

What are you?

17

" The word 'desire'...comes from the Latin *de-siderare*, which means first and foremost to note with regret that the constellations, the *sidera*, do not form a sign, that the gods are not sending any messages in the stars." -Jean-François Lyotard, *Why Philosophize?*

I kept trying to tell you, but I could never get the words out. Each time I tried, my tongue would stay suction-cupped to the roof of my mouth. Each time. Each fucking time. I'll say it now, not for you but for me. Not for you. But for me. Maybe for everyone. I don't really know. Does it matter?

Come closer.

Fine, here goes.

I will die many kinds of death if I don't admit that my eyes have always been too big for my stomach. Living is for me inseparable from having an unfulfillable hunger. Always has been. "As a rule, what you are is one simmering, endless longing."[1]

I will waste away to nothing—die of my hunger—if I don't

admit that what I am is a creature who feels so deeply that I am regularly in danger of dissolution. Same as everyone else. Feeling is for me inseparable from having a deep, spreading ache. Always has been. Same as everyone else.

Are these character flaws, defects? Maybe. Fine, say they are. And?

I still want them.

———

Fill me with your poisons—I now know I'm ready.

We all have to strike a version of the same deal; these defects are not special. I cannot believe I'm unique, or that I'm alone. When a psychic once told me I was psychic, I think this is all she meant. I am contaminated by hunger more than some; I contaminate better than some with my hunger. I have felt everything that each of you has proudly refused to feel. There hasn't been another option. The feelings can't go unfelt. Put this failed philosopher on stage and shame her for saying it, but it will still be true. They cannot go unfelt.

If giving up these defects makes living easier, I will have to resolve to live the hard way. Sometimes that also means the lonely way. "Do you seek warmth of me? Come not too close, I counsel, or your hands may burn. For look! My ardor exceeds the limit, and I barely restrain the flames from leaping from my body!" [2]

This endless simmering is pain, yes, but I am not afraid of pain. I am not afraid of living, is what I mean.

I can see it in your eyes that you're afraid of pain (living). I see it, and I don't like that I see it. There are no gods to show us the way, and you are not okay with it.

I see no traces of who you were that night. When we pulled off our clothing and walked into the water. When the full moon made the water look like milk. When you—emerging from the water—were a god.

My body was beyond itself, but how far? Not far enough, I think. Not nearly far enough.

———

Sometimes when I'm with you, I think, What good has it ever done me to hide the hunger and its effects? It has made me less naked and more dignified, but I've lost most understanding I once may have had of the value of being clothed and decent. It has helped me get by, but it has never done me any good.

The gods and the stars and the forces have no need for clothing. Tell Saturn to be modest. Tell the Milky Way to watch her mouth.

I see now that I have almost always been mistaken when I've thought, as I have too many times, that I was being starved. There has always been more than enough nourishment on offer. Only I have the power to starve myself.

No one starves me but me.

———

I can beg to be spared, can beg on my knees, *please just for tonight*. But it's no use; I would only be begging myself to ignore myself, to watch as I let myself starve.

Some days I can fight it off, it's true. But it results only in temporary starvation. The starvation fixes nothing, resolves nothing, leaves nothing explained. I know well the lesson Lyotard delivers: "you will not evade desire."[3]

Time to give up the ghost. What I desire is *more*. And you don't offer it.

18

It gets worse.

They were all right—each and every one of them—to warn me to stay away from you. But none of them had what I had. They didn't know what it's like to see you on your knees, to see you begging. They didn't know. They still don't.

Once, you slapped my face and said, *Act dumb, you want to survive don't you?* You started giving yourself away with increasing recklessness.

It was easier to hate you when you would not say that you loved me, needed me, had to possess me. You learned new ways to draw me in. I liked watching you learn.

———

Once, I escaped and drove away from you, into the mist, the fall leaves their perfect set of insane flames as everything switched over to decay, and I could feel a new kind of death growing within me. Your amorphous figure back there in the distance, receding, dissolving. You had made the new death in me possible, I understood, and this would bind me to you once again, I could see. Your death growing in me felt too good.

I said it gets worse, didn't I?

––––––

Once, under the stars, deep in the night, I felt ready to welcome you. I said, *Have me have me, take me away, take me all the way.* I will act dumb for you, I want to know I want to see. I will do whatever I have to.

I hated and loved every minute of it. It was exhilarating to show you my soul, to show you all this death drive, not knowing what you would do with it, if I could handle it. You were telling me how much you did not need me, but I also saw you begging. *Felt* you begging, felt it deep inside me, less like surging and more like a sad, slow seeping this time.

Whatever you are, you need a strong swimmer. I am that. I don't get panicky underwater. I slow my heartbeat like the coaches taught me. That night I opened my eyes and saw what I could, in the dark, in the haze; maybe the water was murky, but I opened my eyes and watched you move toward me, nothing discernible but everything palpable. Felt as a new kind of contact happened. I was fileted. I was flayed. I was stretched on the racks, twisting and twisting as you whispered, *Yes that's it baby, yes yes, you feel so good.*

What had I imagined was possible? What did I think could happen—what could be breathed into existence—in that moment of contact?

––––––

Your eyes on me—if that's what they are—breaking me and breaking me. Me thinking, *There is nothing to watch here. No one and no thing—I am not a me, look away away away. There is nothing here. Leave. Leave. Please leave.* For less than a second I thought, *Look at me again and I will chop your fucking head off.*

It dissolved.

———

I knew that I no longer needed you to understand that I existed.
And still, I wanted your apocalypse.

PART 3

19

Go back. And back. And back.

Was there a time when you knew yourself to be capable of everything they said you were not capable of? Was there a time? Did you have dreams? Did you dream of anything?

Deep in that heart-cave—that living, breathing imagination—deep in there, safely hidden: what lived, what still lives? Something small but strong, something curious, watchful. Something quiet and sovereign, something generous and malleable. It is not brittle, not fragile and inflexible.

How did it stay alive?

20

Don't make me do this. You're the only one I don't want to write to. You're probably the only one I need to write to.

First to carry me, first to put me down, first to show me things I wish you had let others show me. First to visit cruelty upon each part of me, because, I suspect—though I will never know—that it was visited upon you day after day, until you knew of no other way to live. First to break my heart and say, *It's a shame you did this to yourself.*

The only recurring dream of my childhood: you are chasing me in circles around a basement furnace with a knife in your hand. Each time I wake from the dream, I am relieved for a split second, because the dream is not real life, only to watch as the relief fades, and a deeper horror sets in, because the dream *is* real life. There is no one I can tell. No one will understand, no one will know how to comfort me, I know, because it's not possible. This legitimate fear for my life will not be comforted away.

You were the earth itself, and you were always killing me.

When the vines gather their strength and band together to choke out the trees, do the trees think, *This must be love?* Is it love? When the moss covers the rocks, do the rocks say, *Thank you, I need you?*

————

I don't know what love is to you. I don't know if you can love. I've been getting better at loving you on what I *think* are your terms, but the fact is that I don't know the terms of love for you. Because I don't know if you can love. If you can, it is a secret.

Is that the kind of thing one is never supposed to say?

Should I read you charitably and say, *Of course you can love, you just don't know how to show it?* No. I shouldn't. It's too dangerous to read you charitably.

As your decay progressed year after year, as everything within you that was killing you picked up steam and strength, I remember being able to count on one hand the number of times I had seen you smile. I began to understand the depth of your sickness, your disease, and the depth of my sadness at never having known you happy or joyful or loving or present. Going mad inside all your laws.

Loving you is like praying to a god that does not exist. Knowing better—avoiding the danger—is not the real issue. The real issue is that selfless love that gives and gives without expecting anything in return is hard, and it hurts. It's a fresh death each day.

And so, you've given me the gift of writing. "To begin (writing, living) we must have death. [...] We must have death, but young, present, ferocious, fresh death, the death of the day, today's death."[1]

You are my daily death. Though I am not yet ready to thank you for it.

Are you blind? Here I am.

Every question I want to ask you is one I cannot ask you.

21

If at first I thought you were people—a person, even—I eventually saw that you were not reducible to anything like an individual. I saw, eventually (did I?), that you were ideas and places and weather patterns and the stock exchange and prisons and every single industry and the way that living creatures are classified, and I saw that you would forever evade me.

The distinctions keep collapsing and reappearing, collapsing and reappearing, coagulating, separating, recombining; it just goes on and on and on.

I saw, also, that you would forever be capable of finding me, surging through me, seducing me, torturing me, wanting to kill me, making me love you. Unless I learned how to do more—so much more—than outrun you, I would never be safe from you.

You exist in an endless series of iterations. You keep spinning out and out and out. Sometimes you take the form of a person and people, but you don't stop there.

———

I escape myself with great regularity, because I cannot bear myself, and my limits go. All the time. They just dissolve. I leave myself. Not even I can comprehend how dangerous this is.

You know this. You see it. You weaponize it—you weaponize me, me against me, through you.

———

If you had asked me years ago to take your hand, I would have. I would have been your Persephone. I would have gone anywhere with you—all the way through for you, done anything for you, no matter how much it would have made me hate myself. I would've done it. You name it, I'd have done it.

I owe it to others to understand you now, to try to understand you now, but I don't know if I can. I'm afraid, and I still want you to hold my hand.

I thought that I liked my life without you—I had the audacity and the naïveté to think that I was without you, somehow—but I see that I was never without you.

The emptiness that existed where you were (are?) permeates. It is a permanent, ineradicable emptiness. Maybe it is me. Maybe you are me. No, erase that. Unthink that. Unfeel that. Unsee that.

Undo it. Undo it, undo it. Can I?

22

I saw you walking toward me down the hall, and your stride alone was enough to let all the other yous fall away. *Oh fuck*, I thought. *Oh fuck oh fuck, use me.*

When I first saw your bare shoulders, I thought I might faint. In your movements, I saw something I had not yet seen: the kernel of sweetness, of delicacy, deep inside the horror. Eventually it would remake my understanding of everything.

I was swimming. I can still access the force of that feeling—how it was so much more than a gaze, than being made real through gaze. And how the surging felt different—just as dangerous, but as though the danger were shared somehow. It was not gentle, necessarily, it was just more everything than it had been before. It was not always nighttime.

Your shoulders were real. It was real flesh and blood. I had not made it up. You were everything in one. You were all yous, every single one of them, human and nonhuman, all of them combined, and yet you were you, a kind of you I had never before known.

Was it possible that you were different? Is it possible still?

I am writing to you now to let you know: you were the trees. You were the sound of the rain in the forest. I had never actually wanted people—I had wanted the forest, I had wanted you. You were the ocean. You were jealousy and hatred and envy and everything delicate, precious, fragile, lovely, breakable. You were you. You were sunlight, you were oxygen, you were moss and flesh-eating bacteria and scummy ponds, you were death and birth and laughter. You were not even a body, but you were. You were very hard. And very soft.

No riddles or rhymes or games—nothing in between.

I wanted to claim something of you and absorb you, take all your animating forces into me. I was no better than the worst of you, I saw, bacterium eating bacterium, just less powerful. How could I have been so blind to myself for so long?

Now that I had seen, could it be different?

———

I wanted you to absorb me. I saw that you saw what was precious in me. I knew that if you were going to kill me, you would kill me quickly, like a skilled hunter. You would use me up just right. My pain was not particularly interesting to you.

You reached for me—it was so plain and brave—and I reached back. It was quiet, so quiet. I thought, for just a moment: *Sometimes things see other things, and not just themselves reflected in things.*

Something happened. I wanted to stay alive.

23

You kept calling out to me. Again and again, no matter how hard I worked to stop hearing, no matter how much I thought my vision had sharpened. You were calling and calling, from inside me sometimes, yes. I could hear, but I couldn't *hear*. I was still too afraid. I couldn't get the right ears to *hear* hear, no matter how hard I tried.

I found myself saying that if I could travel across time, travel through space at the speed of light, at the moment the atom first got its electrons, I would find you. And find you. *I would find you.* If there were a way to find you, I would have found you, found you. You you you. I would give in. I would catch you at your weakest.

I grew up a little, and I pictured a weekend. A long one, even. If only I could have been ready to kill you then. I pictured a nice room and a selection of consciousness-obliterating substances and a room service menu—privacy, but not.

You had been begging for it, after all. I pictured it. And it materialized—all of it—and I did nothing but cry.

You are the places where people go to enact every hidden, silent fantasy—the cruelty and the beauty too—and you are the fantasies themselves, and the economies that shape and regulate them. No, that's crazy. Isn't it?

You are the motel on the side of the highway and the stained sheets on the creaky beds and the dildoes left behind, and you are also the bibles and the mold growing in the corners and the peeling paint in the bathroom, and you are also The Ritz and The Plaza and the fine dining and the top-notch lighting program and the smooth marble of the bar where you place your drink.

No. You are the underpaid bartender with a knowing, world-weary smile and the businessman picking up the fellow lonely traveler and the girl looking uncertain in her dress and also you are the tray of perfect Spanish olives, and you are the people who cannot enter either the bar or The Ritz or even the room at the Super 8. You are the ones left to rot and the ones overseeing the rot. You are their gestures and their clothes and their slow blinks and the rapid firing of their neurons and no.

No. I brought you back. And I stole everything I could from you. I stole it all.

I waited until you were asleep, and I took a 20 from your wallet, but then I realized there was nothing I could buy with it. I did not yet understand.

I wanted to steal more and more, but there was nothing to take. I could empty your pockets forever, I saw, and there would never be anything I could use. It was all so useless.

———

Sometimes I want to play along. I want to see if I can beat you at your game. Let's imagine me on your arm, shall we? Just like you like it—I am beginning to understand. Let's place our bodies at the scene of the crime. What do we see?

Deep breath, baby, I can see you saying. Deep breath baby, in and out in and out, like so many inviting knives—that's all there is. All different sizes and shapes, in all different hands.

24

I ask you, keep asking you, wringing my hands: how?

You say: *Climb into you. Into you as your body. You are this body. But don't do it only from the neck up. This needs all of you.* Like Rilke says, walk deep into yourself, but do it with all of you. Walk deep into yourself with yourself, until you know you're lost. If you wait patiently, even for 20 minutes, you'll end up seeing something.

And then you tell me: if you're lucky and ready, the right ghosts will appear. *Ghosts can take any form, be any thing—keep all your senses peeled. Maybe they've been waiting for you, maybe they will help you see.* Or maybe the ghosts are the ideas themselves. You have to allow yourself to be haunted. *Don't you know this?* you ask me, how did you not know this.

And then, if you don't want to let me go—are you enjoying yourself, I sometimes wonder—you guide me, saying *Once the arrival happens, don't go under with it.* This is what distinguishes you from the most intense high, you remind me. Let them come up to you. You don't need to dive under to them. You are only just barely in charge; wield your authority carefully, like a mother would in the face of a smart three-year-old throwing a tantrum.

They need your nighttime self, you say. *And you need them,* you say to me, *to understand your solitude, to see the contours of it.* You need them to show you what you have refused to let yourself think-feel, what you have swallowed for too long.

They always hit with the same force, and I can do nothing but sit in the dark, silent. *You cannot go on assuming you understand, just because you once did.* You were wrong to think you understood in the first place. You will die one day; wouldn't you like to know that you've attempted the impossible, no matter how small, how insignificant?

When they're substantial, I'm lost in the swirl. It will hurt, I tell myself. I tell myself, because you begin to recede. It will hurt for a long time. It may be difficult to determine what, if anything, is coming, but you've always shown me that eventually, something *is* coming.

When you're nearly done with me, you taunt me, and I am ready to be taunted: *Did you think the good ones, the really life-altering ones,* you say, *the ones that re-shape you could arrive simply and calmly? Did you think they could be placid?* Did you think this was the goal of life? To live calmly, simply, placidly, facing as little discomfort as possible?

———

Some arrivals just aren't suited to sunlight. Some need darkness and solitude and vulnerability to arrive. You keep showing me this.

I have to be willing to be naked. And then even more naked. And more naked still. They have to know—you have to know—that I'm ready.

As with any birth, naked and undignified.

25

Even still, despite your occasional retreat, you are always near. I can never shake you. The toilet tank hisses at me, and it sounds like you. This endless back-and-forth is just exhausting. How much more can I really endure?

Sometimes you're so compelling, I want you to drain me of every last ounce of blood, just so I can see how powerful you'd be with me flowing through you, in my last moments alive. I would take my final breath as I watched you coming into your own, accepting your power, ascension *ad infinitum*.

I am genuinely suicidal when you come around, and always have been, each time. Some part of me wants you to push me toward it. Maybe it would be enough—maybe it would be a good death. *Fuck it. Lead us to the apocalypse.* But there are so many varieties of you—you exist in an endless series of iterations. How quickly you undo all my work. A small fall can do so much damage.

Are you dead? Are you alive?

Once more, because I never know if you've heard me (you give so little indication of having heard anything): are you alive? Do you feel anything? Are you even here?

I am growing new teeth, and I have questions to ask you. One day, I'll be ready.

———

I want to see you running down an empty street at midday.

I want to see you smashing a bottle of wine on a boulder.

I want to see you punching the father of your youth in the face.

I want to see you twirling an elegant woman on a dancefloor.

I want to see you singing at the top of your lungs with your oldest, closest friend.

I want to see you cracking an egg and eating it raw.

I want to see you jumping off the diving board, sailing into the water headfirst.

I want to see you strapped to a gurney, preparing to undergo surgery.

I want to see you crying as you fuck the most beautiful person you've ever known, because you understand that you will never possess anyone.

I want to see you on your knees, because you finally understand how powerless the stealing of power makes you.

26

Watch it, I saw, watch watch watch. You must watch your sight and your hearing, I saw—and be careful what you report. They will laugh, I saw. They will laugh and laugh. There goes the person who thinks she can do it, who's willing to try. There goes the one who wants to see the end of the universe.

There's that one who wants to get the universe out of her, how pathetic. Poor girl.

But this was always going to happen. It would eventually be unavoidable. I knew it all along. I *had known it* all along.

All those times I thought I had cut you out were nothing more than the moments when you left me alone long enough for me to begin understanding you.

27

Back again, back. What was happening?
Maybe it was rock bottom. But it was also childhood.

―――――

I was a teenager trying to live at the speed of escape.

I was trouble that summer at the Christian camp in the mountains, surrounded by the foreign languages of an unknown world, playing along because they said it was good and right, and I knew I was supposed to be good and right. I worked myself into a trance all night long to stay near the boy, the beautiful devout boy who prayed like he meant it. I sang along with the songs I didn't know, confessed to sins that were not sins, I cried and begged for forgiveness for the fact of this flesh, all to be near him, to see with his eyes, to feel his weight and not mine, to see what came next.

It worked, and you were so proud of me—I could feel it. I watched him move closer and closer to me all night, asking me to pray privately with him, his eyes fixed on the tears streaming down my face. And I watched as days later, he was kicked out of morning prayer service, because he was physically incapable of keeping his hands off me.

The other girls thought I had achieved something by capturing his attention, but you and I knew the truth: all I wanted was to get back to that moment of trance, of rapture. When I felt my borders dissolve, when I was beyond the limits of what I could comprehend.

Jesus was not with me in the chapel that night, praying until the sun came up, but you were.

———

I spent another night throwing up, turning myself inside out to expel you. You could not be worth all the trouble. But you were inside all the others too (weren't you?)—why were they so unbothered by it? They were not up all night vibrating with the need to expel you. I couldn't understand it.

I was ready to forget that a myself was possible.

But I returned and returned—why?—tethering a self to a my. Why? I think I liked knowing that someone was listening through the walls. I liked knowing that you might lack control in relation to me, just another thing you were moving through.

Because you seemed to move through me differently than you moved through the others. Because, way in the back of me, I stopped needing to tell myself that one day, you would not move through me.

———

A darkness that belonged to you began to penetrate me. It grew and grew and grew within me. I watched with wonder and confusion as I welcomed it. I said yes. Yes to myself, this terrible thing called self.

Yes to life up to death.

Yes to the pain.

Yes to the blackness, to you.

Yes to the brokenness, the inevitable failure.

Yes to the humiliation.

Said yes, and then: more.

You moved in and out of me with such force, grabbing at my hips, and I said Yes as much as I wanted to. I took it all into me. If I had to contain it all, then fine, I would contain it all. I would get square with the violence of it.

28

Do you remember the night I said yes? Yes and yes and yes again?

Do you? Do you remember that I meant it when I said it? Do you remember how high we were flying? How we were miles and miles up, how it felt that nothing could pull us down, take us down? Do you remember that you finally whispered the words that dissolved me all the way?

I wonder if you can remember anything, if you have what we call a memory.

———

You fly so high. So high it scares me. You perform some death-defying feats, that's for sure. You fly through the air with the greatest of ease, I've seen it. Really, I mean really, you just do whatever the fuck you want.

But I watch you soaring above me, and I think I see that you are sick. I can see it hovering, lingering, following you even as you perform with grace and skill. It's too amorphous to grab hold of, though. I glimpse it, and you see that I've glimpsed it. You hide it, you steal it away, with all the speed and agility one would expect of an acrobat. I keep trying to hold it, to keep it in my arms, but it's impossible to hold; it keeps slipping away. *Kept* trying, maybe I should say. I don't know which tense to use anymore—I can't figure it out.

———

Can you not let yourself admit that what you desire is everything? Maybe you've flown so high for so long that you've lost your ground-legs. Maybe your performances come so naturally that even when naked, you are not naked.

And then there's me, on the other hand. I plunge headlong without the safety of a net, because I just don't know how to perform. You have never plunged headlong without the safety of a net, but I keep falling for the tricks of the show, believing you're actually risking something. I must have known all along, and I must have been lying to myself.

Even as I fell and fell, I could feel you winding tighter around me, coiling up safely inside me.

———

I don't care about clarity or rules. Not now, anyway. Right now, I care about risk. Someone once examined you and said to me, "How often is ambiguity just an excuse to treat someone poorly?" First I thought: no ambiguity? What's the fun in that? Also it's just not possible. Ambiguity is ineradicable. Then I thought: rules are not what I need. Risk is what I need. From me, from you. The trouble is that you're so good at performing risk, I don't know if it's real or not.

Sometimes you ask for a high-flying acrobatic partner, but I know that what you really want is someone to break your fall, whenever it happens. Because it will happen—you know that?

You just want a body under yours. A body for breaking all your falls. Everyone sees that you are special, and they rush to break your fall, imagining any contact with you will be enough. No one stops to wonder if they'll be crushed. Was I just another one of those bodies?

———

I am tired to the bone—beyond the bone—when I think about you. I am tired down to the soul. I have given you everything, sliced myself down the middle, turned myself inside out, asked *Which of these do you need, take them.* Sliced myself and sliced myself and sliced myself.

Silly, stupid, pathetic, naive little me, all I wanted was your heart. I forgot that I was paying upfront for something that would not—could not—exist by the time I was done paying. And I am out of money.

You know what you've shown me? That artistry alone is never enough. And that if there's a person behind or underneath or somehow separate from the artistry, the artist is just a liar. A dangerously skilled liar. You are not living the artistry, you're living a lie. And so, you could never really want the things you say you want. Are you rejecting life? Rejecting yourself? Rejecting love? I believe that you have never taken a risk, never *needed* to take a risk.

All this time, you've been asking if I'm ready to suffer, not knowing what you were asking me, never having risked a thing yourself. *Self*—it's not the right word, I know, but my options are limited here. Language will only get us so far, whatever we are.

I need to say it—this tired body compels me. I don't care how pointless it is. I will waste myself on whatever I must.

"81. What I know: When I met you, a blue rush began. I want you to know, I no longer hold you responsible." My rush with each of you has not been blue. I think it has been black, always black. A surging, sweeping black. I cannot hold you responsible for the things you made happen within me, but the question is: what *can* I hold you responsible for?

———

The surging blackness: how can I be so sad to lose something I've never even had?

It gets darker: what would I not do for you, for the darkness? (Tell me what I wouldn't do. I dare you.) How would I not contort myself to be the object of your desire? How would I not destroy myself in the hopes of becoming and remaining your obsession?

Darker still: I would like to dissolve into the great blackness of the universe. In the face of our denial of each other. I want to evaporate in the face of what each of you has shown me about myself, about the size and capacity of my desire.

The surging blackness *is* the desire itself, and I have no interest in eradicating it. I want to follow it while somehow still remaining here, remaining alive. (There I go saying it.)

You say I have a strong death drive. Imagine me blinking coyly, mocking your certainty that you know my insides, asking: *is this what you mean?* If I keep loving you, I will die.

Who taught you how to love?

PART 4

29

Enough of that.

I looked through my dresser and decided to give away everything you had given me. It was time. Once again, I thought I understood.

I told no one. I knew people would ask if I was suicidal, if they knew what I had done. A warning sign: people give away nice things, things that are supposed to have value and confer meaning. Maybe I was suicidal. I don't know. Was I? Do you remember? Did you care? Would you have cared if I called you, found some way to reach you, and said *Please listen, please help, I want to end me*? I *was* suicidal, and that has not changed.

Maybe I have nothing left to perform.

I didn't stop at the contents of the dresser, though. I gave away the food. The house, too. I gave away the house. And the car. And the children and the husbands—all of them, all ten thousand of them. I gave away everything. I could no longer enjoy it, knowing that it was all composed of the suffering of others, knowing that I was no better than you.

It was a moment of weakness—I could not look into the suffering and accept my responsibility for it. I wanted an easy answer. I wanted to be rid of you, once and for all.

30

There is some lightness in you, some kind of possibility, something that does not always extinguish. The trouble is that it's so hard to access.

Do you hide it? Or is it that I'm incapable of seeing it most of the time?

31

You appear, and I'm naked on the forest floor or swimming somewhere far from land or in the back of the warehouse pleasantly drugged, lights permanently out, or coiled up tight in the palm of something, some kind of *something*. You appear, and I'm electricity, ready to be put to use by you.

If it's dark enough, you know I'll do whatever you like. I don't need the darkness, but it makes it easier.

They warn me to stay away from you, but their warnings are mostly worthless, because they've never tried to understand you. They give me a list of rules to follow if I am to engage with you. They tell me precisely how to behave, what to say, what to wear, what to think of what to dream of how to hold my body. But none of them know how good it feels, or *that it even feels* to be in the dark with you. But oh it feels, it feels like everything. I can't expect them to understand. How could they?

———

The last time, I brought you the good drugs, and I laid myself out in front of you, hoping to pacify you, to let you think you'd won. It didn't work. You were more perceptive than I'd realized.

I felt irreparably unsafe in your arms. I was in the ocean again. I did not want that to change. There was no exchange possible—there was nothing you could offer to neutralize how unsafe I was. I did not want that to change.

From deep inside me, you hissed in my ear, *Who can really say how much of our desire is predicated on being the object of someone else's desire?* and I felt your pulse in mine. My intestines told me a truth, and I had to hide it from you. I could feel it glowing in me.

32

It was you who taught me that there are places that are both living and not, and that because of this, they love and hate themselves in equal measure.

It's a long way from Chicago. From that Jewish suburb, that enclave of chemically-straightened hair and noses broken in order to erase jagged lines.

It's a long way.

———

You wear grey and damp and sad so well. The fog hangs in the alleys, as though it belongs there. In the low, misty light, the eyes of all strangers are beautifully menacing. Nothing is for me here, and that is fine. Better, even.

No description is better than Pamuk's: "I love the overwhelming melancholy when I look at the walls of old apartment buildings and the dark surfaces of neglected, unpainted, fallen-down wooden mansions; only in Istanbul have I seen this texture, this shading. When I watch the black-and-white crowds rushing through the darkening streets of a winter's evening, I feel a deep sense of fellowship, almost as if the night has cloaked

our lives, our streets, our every belonging in a blanket of darkness, as if once we're safe in our houses, our bedrooms, our beds,
we can return to dreams of our long-gone riches, our legendary
past. And likewise, as I watch dusk descend like a poem in the
pale light of the streetlamp to engulf these old neighborhoods, it
comforts me to know that for the night at least we are safe; the
shameful poverty of our city is cloaked from Western eyes."[1]

———

I have always loved places that reflect our ability to only just
barely manage decay. Controlled rot is always beautiful. I love
cheese for the same reason. But you are something else.

It was strange to me that I began to pass for Turkish only
after I knew I could not stay with you for much longer. But it
makes sense: if I was finally an Istanbullu, it was only because I
was unsure of whether or not I should be there.

My eyes were foreign, after all, and though it was not the
poverty that made me want to shame you, I wanted to shame
you nonetheless. Even though I loved you.

I hated seeing hüzün[2] in everyone's eyes, because it was a
reminder of the inevitability of decay, and the sadness that
accompanies it. It was a reflection—you were a thousand
mirrors, 20 million mirrors that stared right back at me. "For
when they gaze into a colorless image, they see their melancholy
confirmed."[3]

It was more than just that, though. It was a hint of what may
be coming—what long-term, seeping, spreading hüzün does to
a people. I had never in my life been assaulted in so many ways
by so many different people in such a short time. I lost track of
the violences, minor and major, after the fifth ass-grab, the sixth
Cover your hair arm-pinch, the cab ride with the driver who
wanted to show me what he knew of *American sluts like in the
gangster movies*, he said—a potentially terrible death that I

somehow narrowly escaped. I wondered what else hüzün could do, would do.

———

I understood, if only just a little, what I saw when I saw the eyes of the men fishing from the bridge. It's a fact that I saw fewer women, especially in the older parts of the city, but when I saw them, and they were curious or brave enough to raise their eyes, I saw it even stronger.

This aspect of you agreed with me. I met it, and I wanted to keep meeting it. I saw it as a kind of honesty, a condition of being resigned to living through history. The weakness in me fought it sometimes, wanting to believe it was possible to live outside of history. But the rest of me said, *Thank you for not hiding it.*

You showed me that there is no outside.

———

Move halfway across the globe, and suddenly you are almost none of the things you have always been. The disorientation. The rudderlessness. The exhilaration. The exhaustion. You're a helpless child, someone with elementary communication skills, a wide-eyed stumbling wanderer.

Even still, meeting you is an experience unlike any other. "In a few minutes I would open the door and escape into the city's consoling streets; and having walked away half the night, I'd return home and sit down at my table and capture their chemistry on paper." The difference between the two of us, however, is that you and your streets were not consoling for me, nor did they offer the easy and pleasurable thrill of the exotic; they were threatening, despite the times I escaped in them. And I was not yet capable of understanding their chemistry.

I had too much living to do, in the years after you, to understand *what* I had seen and felt and come to know.

The life I had in you is so remote to most people here that they don't even ask about it. *How glamorous*, they'll say, if they say anything at all. It is still a place so foreign that most Americans don't know which language I had to learn upon moving there. So foreign—so far from consideration—that most people I talk to about you confess that they didn't know you exist on two continents.

I can share details and play world-traveler, travel writer, sophisticated wanderer, but it is only play. I can talk about the apartment and its crumbling rooftop with a view of the Hagia Sophia and the Sea of Marmara, I can talk about the bakkal on the corner with the perfectly thin and flaky yufka and the shop owners who always insisted on offering tea, even if they knew I wouldn't (couldn't) make a purchase, and the olives and the pide and the dürüm and the camel wrestling and the way the streets all turned sharp, sudden corners, and the sounds of tavla players in the cafes below our apartment, and the smell of bodies on the subway, because deodorant was a Western decadence at the time, and how shocking I found the difference between tony, shiny Nişantaşı and our neighborhood on the edge of Taksim and Cihangir, with its clandestine gay bathhouses, and the calm, perfect quiet of the Yerebatan Sarnici first thing in the morning, before the tourists arrive, and you're so far underground you can't hear the incessant noise of the city above. But that's about all I can do.

When really: I remember the evening call to prayer surging through my entire body as I sat on the roof drinking rakı, watching the birds hover above, vibrating out of myself. I remember the smell of sewage lingering everywhere, reminding me daily of death and decay. I remember feeling so full—so saturated—with experience that I wasn't sure if I was still alive.

I don't trust my ability to communicate the profound untetheredness that occurred as I began to live in a new language in a new place, because it also demanded that I have a new body and a new life. With only strangers around. Your strangers. Strangers with those melancholy eyes. So I am mostly silent about it.

———

One day, I was sitting outside in the rain, and I felt it descend. I was with a friend. We had just eaten the meal of a lifetime in Kadiköy. We were smoking and drinking tea underneath the awning, watching the rain fall and the people rush by. Despite all this—the life-affirming meal, the pleasure of speaking in English with a friend, the gentle rainfall, the brisk pace of every-thing—hüzün came in low and slow, returning me to myself, whispering: sorrow can never be outrun.

As always, you blinked in response. The men on their stools in the cafe below the apartment saw it in my eyes and said, *Girl, feed your husband raw honey to make his dick stronger, then you'll have babies, you'll begin to live.* You'll be like the mother cat with her litter of kittens, too busy feeding them to think. I nodded, amazed that I understood them, that my Turkish had progressed.

———

Your hüzün is portable, and I still carry it with me. My own personal hüzün is a living, changing, growing being, just like yours.

Every time I cannot communicate what it felt like to conduct my first real conversation, every time I hear that another section of the city has been cleared of its co-ed cafes and its bookstores that breed immorality, every time I think of what it was like to wander the backstreets of Çukurcuma with only a pen and a notebook in my bag, every time I consider that I might never make it back to you, and that even if I do, it and I will be mostly unrecognizable, I *am* hüzün.

"My starting point was the emotion that a child might feel while looking through a steamy window. Now we begin to understand *hüzün* not as the melancholy of a solitary person but the black mood shared by millions of people together. What I am trying to explain is the *hüzün* of an entire city: of Istanbul."[4]

People like to imagine themselves globalists—sophisticated world-travelers—until they live abroad, and they are the object of derision or dismissal, until they encounter a melancholy they cannot explain away. In my memories, the globalists were always gathered in clusters at their impressive parties, missing home, dreaming of home, clucking their tongues at the barbaric local customs, as they looked through me, because I dared to say that I suspected your customs were not any more or less barbaric than the ones *at home*.

I felt compelled to defend you, because I had fallen in love with you. But I recognize that love is not enough, not nearly enough. I should never have been at those parties.

———

I wandered your streets every day, seeing you, feeling you, breathing you, hoping to understand you. I was not a flaneur—it was not a category available to me—but I began to see that the flaneur *must* feel melancholy. How could one wander the streets —any streets—and not absorb the profound sadness of existence? A sadness that we can only sometimes paper over with pleasant smiles and polite nods. But not when you're strolling through the ruins of a lost empire; it's just not worth the effort. There are too many starving children. And they kept starving, no matter how many times I fed them.

You taught me that hüzün merely returns us to ourselves. And that we are all living amongst the ruins of a lost empire, even if we are lucky enough to forget it.

33

I have this earth, and I know I have no right to ask for anything else. This also means that I have you, whatever there is to be had, in whatever capacity. There is one thing I can do—one thing and one thing only: drive my hand into the dirt. I drive my hands into the dirt, because I get nothing else.

I miss the way I used to believe you could breathe me into existence. I have to do it on my own now. It's a little bit lonely.

Please don't let me be bitter. I don't want it to be brittle. I want it elastic and malleable. This pain in my chest is the only thing you've really given me, and I still love it. I still treasure it— evidence that I exist, evidence that this hell is just life, nothing more, nothing less.

———

Once, I saw you search my face for meaning—you who for so long said I offered none. I saw your eyes, or whatever they are, scanning me, slowly and then rapidly, looking for the right way to respond—you who said there was nothing outside of you, nothing you could come to know from anyone or anything else. I saw it. I know that I saw it. And I felt it, felt it with great force.

I can take a lot. So much. I just take it and I take it. I get off on how much I can take. It needs to end.

I share some responsibility here. I am not blameless. Maybe I don't even blame you. I still want you gone. I want you gone I want you gone I want you gone. If I lied and promised never to love anything else, never to see promise in anything other than you, if I agreed to let you chain me to the wall in your basement for three weekends a year, could I be done with you?

No. No, of course not. There is no possibility of abandoning the struggle.

———

I walked through the woods, and I thought of you—these endless forms, more than I could ever count—and I thought about how sometimes everything in this world seems to be snapping like twigs underfoot. For a brief moment, I wished to light myself on fire. It passed.

Why do we value potential? Why do we care about the thing called potential? Why have I allowed myself to be invested in anything, anyone? Or in understanding you.

It's all wrong, it's been all wrong for so long. I'm embarrassed that I don't have the words, but it's true—I just don't have the words. Do words have potential? Is this why I try to find them?

I wanted to shout at you, *Tell me what you can't tell me, find a way, figure it out. Speak your ability to speak into existence. Speak it. Speak it into existence.* I have been waiting all this time.

Say that you live to hear me say it. Say it. I want the saying. I want it want it want it.

Say that you live to hear me say anything. If there are no answers, at least say that you live to hear my voice reminding you of it.

I know that you are living, that you are life itself, even if I can't identify you, can't name you. I know that you are living. I can feel it.

PART 5

34

It will take a lifetime, but this is what I will tell myself: do it wrong. DO IT WRONG. You've never done it right, anyway. Forget that you ever learned there was a right way to do it. (Do I have any other options?)

Be illegitimate. You've never been legitimate, anyway. Anyone who confers legitimacy will only use you to build a new form of legitimacy, to fool us all into thinking that legitimacy really exists.

I am too tired to endure the important people and their importance. I can't do it anymore.

DO IT WRONG. Keep the error. Keep it and hold it close. No gods, no masters; it's errors all the way down.

"I had to stop behaving 'like a literature person,' like a woman, I had to stop telling stories, I had to be no one in particular, I had to erase my 'I,' my gender, my character, my history, my story. I had to use that awful neuter, asexual language you find in dissertations and theses. I had to write in the style of those introductions to papers or dissertations on the works of great thinkers written by administrators. As Irigaray says quite rightly, even now, 'because women have no language sexed as female,' they use a language that is a 'so-called neuter language where in fact they are deprived of speech.' They are not at home in this language; they do not have the 'words that would allow them both to get out of and return to their homes. To 'take off' from their bodies, give themselves a territory, an environment and invite the other to some possible share or passage.'"[1]

———

I should have said this to you years ago. I wanted to be yours. I really did. But my head and my heart are whores. One of your most important representatives saw it, took a long hard look at me and said, *Your body is an outlaw*, and not even I understood just then how right he was. But he was right, wrong as he was about most everything else. Goddamn right this body is an outlaw. A defector.

Apologies can be defenses; defenses can be apologetic. I attempt a defense that is not apologetic. Simultaneously, I attempt an apology that is not defensive. I admit that I don't know of a metric for success for this endeavor.

I'm attempting the impossible.

Everything has a degree of impossibility, you know.

———

I want to think of Bataille. Like Bataille weeping at the thought of Nietzsche, I crumble when I imagine Bataille seated at his desk. (Would he have had a writing desk? What a stupid question.)

I can glimpse, and grasp, for one distinct second, what he means when he says we have to set the universe as the measure of our lives. I *am* "the explosive character of this world," in human form.[2] I don't exist to survive—we don't exist to survive —because existence is not an end; I exist only temporarily as one more moment of expenditure throughout the universe.

My existence is just an unintended temporary consequence

of a few wasteful moments. Maybe it frees me. Maybe that freedom slips away.

———

What am I doing? How dare I, I know. I am collaborating with you. Reclaiming a subjectivity, a form of existence that is other and more. I'm taking off, not sneaking away.

You couldn't touch me now if you tried. Now I am nameless, faceless, formless, hopeless, homeless—that is, finally at home.

———

There is fear, though. It finds me. I won't turn away from it. *Be afraid. Do it anyway.*

"And I should now put this forward: more than truth, it is fear that I want and that I am seeking: that which opens a dizzying fall, that which attains the unlimited possibility of thought."[3]

I have to seek the dizzying fall, feel the fear of falling, go there with myself.

Falling feels like dying, but it is not dying. Maybe you don't see the difference between the two.

Watch me go—I'm going, just as Malabou did: "As my thinking develops I am un-marrying, de-coupling, divorcing myself a little from philosophy. I am thought absolutely, thought isolated, absolutely isolated. I cross the philosophical field in an absolute solitude. And so now there are no more limits, no more walls, nothing holds me back. It's my only chance."[4]

Can you imagine her fear, and how she must have given into it, feeling the bottom drop out, understanding only her "absolute solitude"? I suspect you cannot.

It was her only chance.

35

You came in close, grabbing me tight, seeing with your eyes (eyes?) that I had seen what I'd seen; and clutching me to you, you told me to swing for the fences.

Nodding into the distance, you said, *It's your world, baby—go.* But you neglected to mention whose fences—*which* fences I was meant to swing for. Yours were the only real ones for you, I saw. How you gave yourself away there.

Be careful, whatever you are. I am watchful as water now.

36

I can show you the way, you said. *I can make things happen for you. I can take you all the way.*

I gave you no answer. I went to bed early. I hibernated. I waited.

37

You write at 1:04am to say,

Remember when I got too drunk to dance in Istanbul? I woke up to you and your friend jumping on the bed around me, trying to rouse me back to the party. I wish I would have rallied and danced. I think of that time like a scene in one of my favorite books, and I want to go back there. I want to be there again, to be there more than I was when I was there. Some part of me feels the need to rectify my past inattentiveness by living larger, more dangerously, more intentionally. Isn't it sad?

Then at 1:20,

But if it wasn't so sad, it wouldn't be beautiful. Nothing can be had, can it? My main man Cormac McCarthy said it best: "beauty and loss are the same thing." To pretend otherwise is to be successful. Easier to hold a river in your hands.

4 minutes later,

I've been listening to Kendrick Lamar's DAMN for a few days straight.

I wake up at 5:30 to the sing-songy shouting of birds in the spring, reading your words, wondering if I'm a fool for thinking I've ever had anything—any beauty—for a moment or two. Or worse: have I been lying to myself? Just how much have I been lying to myself?

We could argue about it, but we won't. We'll just keep talking. Please tell me we'll never stop talking. Tell me if I'm lying to myself. Please.

I write you back to say,

I will hold onto the hope, foolish though it may be, that I've held beauty in those moments when I think I've held it. Yes, it evaporates. Yes, it's never mine to keep. But I get to dance with it for a minute. Like a fool in her apartment in Istanbul, drunkenly celebrating Christmas with some other fools, only to remind themselves that they—some of them, anyway—are from the same strange place called America. They are lonely for things they've never even cared for. They've lost them and they want them back, so they get drunk and dance, stupidly, hoping to lure it all back. But I guess the loss is always part of the beauty. Can we only be still enough to see something and love it if we know it won't stick around for long? What a bunch of ingrates. We can't trust anyone who says they have no regrets, can we? It's the lie of the successful. But I remember that night in Istanbul differently. I was worried that us idiots, us brats not facing down death everyday were dancing around, interrupting the sleep of someone doing something we couldn't imagine doing and had no right to fuck up with our pointless celebrat-

ing. I remember feeling frivolous. I don't know what you
know. And you can't show me what you know.

And the truth is that,

Our years-long correspondence is proof of both my point
and yours. We both know how rare understanding is, how it's
tied to that feeling of existing in some full way—a way that
doesn't demand rectifying past inattentiveness with throwing
existence around or *living larger*. We share a fundamental loneliness. When you send me one of those middle-of-the-night
emails, and I respond with all the honesty I've got, the moments
come into being, they materialize. We are seen. We are understood. We are capable of understanding. It's a river in our hands.
For half a second.

And then it is not.

————

Years later, a fracture in our communication. An irreparable
injury, it seems. You cannot call me back to you. For this reason, I
am unkind, unloving, a real bitch.

I cannot give you anything you want. You hate me for it. You
hate me with all the force of you—I can feel it twisting in me. I
hadn't known that you wanted more, so much more. I thought
everything I had given you was enough. How could it not be
enough? How can all of it not be enough? The love is real, always
has been. I feel trapped, hunted.

Your damn conviction, you write. *You've always had it. That
damn conviction, that damn dark mass of curly hair. How did we
meet?* you ask. *There is no beginning I can think of,* you say.

I feel exposed, but I don't think it's me who's been exposed.
It's the version of me that has lived in you. *Conviction?* In me? No,
not really. I don't think so. Tenacity, maybe. Strength, yes,
sometimes.

Of course I remember the night we met. I remember what

you were wearing, I remember the exact way your hands pushed your glasses up your nose, I remember the smell of Old Spice on you. I remember the bagel you bought for me, because it was 10:00pm and I was hungry and out of money. I remember your smile, your watchful eyes, your stillness. I remember that for days after, I wore the same shirt I'd been wearing that night, because your smell clung to it. There is always a beginning, and it is always composed of the details—material and immaterial—that make up every encounter. Have you mythologized us? Danger lurks there.

Who has lived with you for all these years? Someone with conviction, with dark hair, with an endless supply of love that you can claim whenever you like, with a set of attributes that I think may be alien to me.

I turn the question back on myself, and it gets ugly. Who has lived with me for all these years? Someone satisfied with all the love I can give, across many distances. Someone with that same calm stillness, that same impossibly large presence, that concern for others. Have I been stuck at the beginning for all these years? Have I mythologized us?

You were right, and I am having trouble admitting it. Even I am a river in my hands.

I am stepping away now, leaving the grasping to others. I don't need it anymore—*can't* need it anymore. I don't need your story that sadness equals beauty.

———

I have some words now, and I'm beginning to see that having words is the opposite of romance.

Yes, nothing can be had. That's not particularly beautiful.

38

I stay quiet and small, and resignation arrives. But I am not resigned to you, or to you within me. I am resigned to me, that to be a me requires somehow being with you. It makes you less inside me.

I don't know how it's possible. Maybe you grew tired of me? I no longer have the world, and somehow that gives me a world. I can't quite explain it.

The space where you were grows and grows, and I think it is no longer emptiness itself. I think it might be care. I think it might be the place from which I care.

Yes, I'm a fool, but I'm not that kind of fool. I know what I'm doing: washing dishes in a sandstorm, building a house in a flood zone, singing in my best voice to a room full of deaf school-children. You still growing inside me, or me growing in you, or both. They say it's either bloom or decay, but we both know it's both, always.

———

Every last one of them lied to me about you. They didn't mean to lie—I know they were just reporting what they knew, but it was not enough for me. They did not know what I had. They did not have what I have. Maybe they are to blame, not you, not us.

There are some kinds of intimacy I cannot expect anyone to understand. No one can help me make sense of them.

I'm not saying that I'm *healed*, that I'm whole. Deception is still sometimes the law of the land here, and I like it. *I like it*. What does that tell you about me? You didn't know I was capable of it, did you? I hid it. I hid it well. You don't know the half of it, baby. You never did.

39

No more of your words. No more. I am not saying all language is violence, no not at all. I believe other relations are possible. It's *your* words I can have no more of.

No more? Why? Because you have only ever used them to harm me and everyone like me and everyone worse off than me. *In the name of truth*, you say. *In the name of beauty*, you say. *In the name of all that's good*, you say. In the name of life overall. Maybe I don't want life, then.

Maybe life is nothing more than being subject to your bullshit. (Haven't I been through this before? How many times do I have to do it?) Then I want out. I want out.

———

There will be no more fun for you to have if I'm all the way out, so you keep it just okay enough for me to remain.

But I see it, and I will short-circuit it. Or die trying. *And* die trying.

I see that you'll be bitter about it, and that I'll have to absorb that too. I'm starting to wonder if there's nothing I won't have to absorb. The more interesting question: now that this is half-understood (*wondering about* is halfway to understanding), what becomes possible?

What can be made, and what can be made to happen, if I accept this absorption as inevitable?

40

I began to feel your heartbeat in me. I began to feel it as my own.

There are too many of you to name. But some of you stand out. My gratitude can only be expressed in my living. I believe you wouldn't have it any other way.

You showed me everything there is to know—it was only ever a question of whether or not I could understand you as you showed me.

What happened is that you showed me that there is no Art and Not Art. Only an anemic, dying conception of art and of life can divide and conquer in the ways we've become accustomed to. Our only job is to live into the art-work, to make our lives the works of art that serve as the evidence for the inseparability of life and art, Art and Not Art, all that shit.[1] And not in any kind of self-aggrandizing way. Only in the way that brings us (me) closer to you. Closer to being you, maybe.

———

I am coming face to face with as many as I can. The forces. You appear in them, and I see the beauty there, untouchable, but knowable, maybe. There is something bright in the darkness.

I am coming to understand just how alone I am in the facing. You remind me that I must do this, and that I must accept how unpredictable the results are.

But the results hardly matter, once you get started. It's the dice throw: it's not *good* because you might *win*; it's necessary, because no matter the results, you've thrown—you've risked. It is its own reward.

It's the throwing that matters. You remind me, and there is no condescension in the utterance. I don't think I hear you calling me *Baby*: once you start throwing, you can start living. The possible results fade from view. They won't tell you much about yourself, anyway. Only the solitude of the throwing, the work, can show us ourselves.[2]

———

There is evil in you, though, even when I can't see it or feel it. It's still there.

I have to transmit—I accept this—but now it is clear that I must also transmute.

When I have followed you into the darkness with my trans-mutation instincts turned off, there has been no liberation. Instinct, intuition—whatever it is—it's not lying.

41

You open a bottle of wine. You sit down. You look right at me. *Do you know the muses?* you ask.

I'm not sure, but I might.

We talk about what it means to keep them close. What it means to receive them with grace. How not to anger them with arrogance or a lack of concern. We may never know what they want from us, other than care and attention. They don't seem fickle, necessarily, but they are never ours to keep, and this we know. We remain in their debt, but it's not necessarily a lopsided relationship. They just know when they're being taken for granted.

You say you wonder if you can keep them around when you engage them in the haphazard way you sometimes do. Will they mistake your occasional silence and your intense flings with them for denial, withholding, game-playing? Is it possible that muses can get their signals crossed? I know that if miscommunication is possible, it will occur. But does this apply to muses? Or are they wiser than us and our creations?

I have never lived without them. Not yet, anyhow. They've been particularly good to me lately. I have put in the time, the work. It still feels like a gift— like love—and it brings just as much fear as love. What if they awake one morning and realize I'm a sham? What if they find themselves drawn to someone more interesting, because surely—we all know it—the more interesting person always exists? Is my love and care enough to keep them close?

———

Do they want our genuflection? Or is that insulting to them— behaving as though we could flatter them into paying us attention, assuming that they need or want our pathetic offerings? And what are we to do, when we think they're asking us to do something we've never done before, and that carries with it certain risk? Do we take the risk, trusting that they know better than we do?

You said, *You better keep it weird, you better go where they tell you to—how else will you be able to live with yourself?* I nodded inside myself.

All I know is that *they know* that our thinking and creating are bound by the kinds of lives we're living, and that the lives we live are bound by the thinking and creating we do. They see it when we're slipping from this, and only they can decide whether or not it's worth the trouble to return us to ourselves, via creating, via living.

Once you said to me that your only job was to read into my words to find clues to help you understand me enough to steer me back toward myself. You said to me, *You're a good steady driver, hon, you just need to not let go of the wheel.* In a crucial sense, then, you were my muse. Or that other time you said, *Please stop gesturing at things, waving in their direction, without actually saying them. You've got to hit harder.*

You had decided that I—and whatever I was creating—was worth the trouble. I owe you nearly everything for that decision. You were showing me how to live.

I am trying to land blows, trying to live, hoping the muses see the intensity of my efforts.

42

Time slows when we light a joint and take our clothes off and play the music as loud as it goes. It stays slow and gets slower—swimmingly slow—for a while, for a crucial while, until we are plunged back into the flow and the momentum of living for the work that makes living possible.

There's just that one window, so small, so quick to close. The loneliness returns.

———

Sometimes I imagine that I've achieved calm clarity, but usually I have not.

Sometimes I still allow myself the fantasy of imagining you dying alone, unwanted and alone. ODing on something you didn't even want but were powerless to turn down. But I know you don't die. No part of you, any of you, ever dies. I keep watching as my learning to live makes you wish even harder that I were dead. But you never die, you never do.

I let down my guard for two minutes, and you drag me back to the pit.

I want to be gone, I want to be done, done with this. No, no I don't. Sometimes the wrong thing wishes for death.

———

Sometimes I still want to feel your intensity sweeping through every part of me, wringing me out, leaving me to die on the floor, alone. I have tried every method I know to explain you away, to feel you away. It no longer matters, I think.

Maybe we wanted something from each other. Did we want something from each other? Did we want to reach the other side, together? Did we? Did we want to drown together, to end it all? Did we want to know what it's like to submit?

Did you imagine that you might find in me some limitless pleasure? Blooming in my organs, snaking through my sockets, coiling and waiting, waiting everywhere? Could this body be the source of more you? Could this body be that pleasure?

———

I wanted to survive—I'm just like every other living thing—but also I did it from love, *for* love. I didn't know what love was. Now I'm starting to know what it is, but I know I did it from love, from my small but growing understanding of it. I can hold this fact close. Your love is bullshit—has always been bullshit—and I know this. I wanted it anyway. I wanted your bullshit anyway. Wish me dead again and again, it will not matter. Because if you live through me, we end as one. We end together.

All these years, you have whispered in my ear: *Are you ready to suffer?* But I swear to god swear to god swear that you know nothing of suffering. The persistent asking gives away the not-knowing. Wish me dead if you must—it won't matter, because I will start asking myself. Am I ready to suffer?

Back to the beginning: I know you. I love you. You are in me, and maybe maybe just maybe you are me. The question is, how do I feel the love-hate I feel for you and continue existing? With bitterness, you once seemed to say, *I bet it takes years to learn how to fuck you*, and I shrugged in response, as if to say, *Yeah probably*.

Maybe I regret every time I have fallen in love.

PART 6

43

If life makes us drunk, I think, I don't want life. I don't want the kind of drunkenness that locks us into our own heads, makes it impossible to see each other. I don't want life to be the sensory deprivation of drunkenness. If I want life's drunkenness, I want it to be the kind that slows me all the way down while keeping me aware, draws me down into myself, letting me look straight into you, unflinching, exposed, comprehending. I want a fullness of experience that mostly doesn't track with drunkenness. I want to look straight into you. I want the most sober fucking you've ever known.

Mostly it's the fucking you offer. Because fucking is never just fucking. There doesn't even need to be fucking for there to be fucking. If it's especially useless, especially gloriously wasteful, there *shouldn't* be fucking.

Make me feel equal to life. No, that's the Anaïs talking. And I am not her.

Anaïs says, "When he first stepped out of the car and walked towards the door where I was waiting, I saw a man I liked. In his writing he is flamboyant, virile, animal, magnificent. He's a man whom life makes drunk, I thought. He is like me."[1]

———

No, Anaïs, I don't want what you want. I want someone to make me feel equal to death. *Make me equal to death*, I'll say, or you'll say, or we'll say together, because we know how much everything hurts. Hurts like death.

It will hurt when we touch. It will hurt when we part. It will hurt when we think of each other. It will hurt when we remember, it will hurt when we move on. It will hurt to reunite. It will hurt it will hurt it will hurt. It will always hurt. The pain will have to be part of the pleasure. You said, *To be longing is to be living, baby.* I said, *I am not your baby and I never will be, don't call me that again.*

I wanted to say: let me occupy the space between your pen and your mind, your self (whatever there is of it) and your evidence of it. Hold me in that place. Your hands on me will be the shortcut between those realms. "Where the hand becomes entirely thinking, gentleness begins there too, secretly."[2] Make your hand the thing that thinks on the surface of my skin. Make your hand that which contemplates me in the moment of contact. And then write me into existence.

———

You've taught me that pleasure can be mysteriously fabricated and then elongated, over various distances, and minute by minute, and especially when the pleasure on offer is always on the verge and almost never to be made additionally real by the meeting of bodies. Who cares about bodies, anyhow?

But you have also taught me that there will never be a substitute for skin meeting skin. Somehow, flesh is flesh. Nothing else is flesh. It's unimaginable, isn't it? Bodies meet, and there's no turning back. No other high compares. We reach something unreachable—something inhuman, unhuman, ahuman—and then we are returned to ourselves, nothing more than flesh.

And what is doing the meeting to begin with? Is it something like, You-I approaches I-You and collision occurs, creating a temporary You-I/I-You fusion, but calling it a We would be too stable, too permanent? Can the intensity be maintained? For how long? Does it have to be a high, or can it be the new foundation, the new fundamental state of things? How does that change life, if it sustains?

———

You ask me how many speed freaks I've known, as though I keep a running tally.

I eat the world—*Open open*, you've said, and I've listened—and I eat it and eat it, and it keeps leaving a bitter taste in my mouth. Replace it with something else, if even for a second. I'll always be in trouble though, won't I? Won't I won't I, because I see that I love your bitterness.

"When I say I love him sensually, I do not altogether mean that; I love him in many other ways—when he is laughing at the movies, or talking very quietly in the kitchen; I love his humility, I love his sensitiveness, the core of bitterness and fury in him."[3]

———

You'll speak it straight into me, into the core of me, and your bitterness alone will be enough to turn me inside out. You'll let go of control, because you'll know you're in the presence of something entirely new to you. Me. I will be entirely new to you. Each time. I'll never demand your control—never demand that you give it up in exchange for me—but you'll understand eventually that you have to give it up and let something more powerful take its place. I want to give this to you.

He is like me, as Anaïs says, but not because we both love life.

If you can make me equal to death, you can bring me back to life. Death is the only moment in which I will fully possess myself— my death is the only thing that will ever be only mine.[4] And I as the possessor will be gone the very moment when I can possess it. *Bring me here.* I will pray to this and only this. It is why I am, whatever *I* can be found here.

———

There is no writer here. Maybe a swimmer, someone who wants to go under. And yet. Henry to Anaïs: "The core of you is a writer. And the writer is living."[5] Remind me that to be living—that is, to be writing—is to be facing death.

If we feel equal to life, it is only because we are equal to death.

Remind me, in whatever momentary union can be managed, that death and the loss of these temporary pseudo-selves is all we have. It's the music to which we unite, the funeral dirge to which we fuck—how could it be any other way?

———

Take everything you want from me. Take it all. There is enough of something like a core here to sustain, to live, despite all the taking. I want you to take it. I need to be consumed to continue finding myself. I have enough integrity to be thrown around for a while. Throw me.

Throw me around. I have always had your number, baby. I have always understood the games, the sickness, the swirling darkness, the need to swallow me up like bacterium eating bacterium; I have wanted all of you not just despite but also because of it. I didn't even need to *try* to play the fool; you saw what you wanted to see.

Our desires reveal everything about us. And they need to be re-shaped.

―――――

You've made me long for nothing more than to be reduced to the object of your desire. Yes, to be an object is the thing. Isn't it? To be one's thing is the thing I need most. Reduce me to thinghood, make me your victim, remove me from the useful *order of things*. Remove me from all that is mundane; return me to the most mundane.

Then: watch me, I'm going. I'm going with or without you. Crossing over into some other realm I cannot make sense of or understand in advance. But there's no doubt that I'm going. Not even I can stop myself. *Gone gone gone, gone beyond beyond, hail the goer.*[6] Here I go, there I was—you see me, don't you? You have brought me here, partially—you and the body and the mind and the force and the nothingness that is you, throwing me, consuming me—and you know it. You were never enough.

But I am going. In fact, I am already gone.

44

Let's place our bodies at the scene again. Bodies?—is that even what they are? Who cares.

There's something beautiful in your ability to evade. I see it best with my eyes closed. You resist all forms of capture. Especially language. You evade language with the force of the forces that created it.

You evade your creations (co-creations?) with the force of the forces that explode them big-bang them into existence.

With you, I am like a woman in Hollywood. There's no glamour; forget that, wipe it from your mind. With you, I am like a woman in Hollywood who swears she won't be one of the ones to get a new face, new body, new psyche if she makes it—really makes it—but by the time she's made it, so many sacrifices have been made—so many concessions to the industry and its aesthetic and its expectations that it's too late, it's already begun, before the knife ever comes out. The knife and the needle just finalize the transformations that have been ongoing, slowly and quickly, internally, for years, maybe decades. It's not for me to say whether it's good or bad. I just know that I am subject to the same powers and pressures and forces, and I hate it, and it's you who's done it. I hate it hate it and start to love it with all of me. It's a compression, a process like being made into meat-sludge and pressed into a disc wrapped in plastic and stacked on some refrigerated shelf.

———

Back to the bodies. I am ready to imagine it. I am on your arm again. I'm wearing the dress you want me to wear, my shoulders back the way you like, my hair to one side just like you like. With my lips against your ear, I say *Fuck I'm so high*, in a tone that suggests a promising lack of self-control, because I know it's exactly what you want to hear. I am ready to let you chop me into pieces, because I know how to keep leaving and returning.

Is this fun? I wonder. It is something.

I don't even need you to want it anymore. I have learned, like every galaxy, to be the producer recycler destroyer of all energy. I am dangerously self-contained, self-sustained. *Potentia gaudendi* ad infinitum.

You are the force that will eventually make the Milky Way and Andromeda collide, but no matter, baby, so am I.

———

You look at me funny, I feel it in me, and I see that what's happening is, I can get behind and underneath you, and it begins to unnerve you—what am I? You start wondering, though you have never wondered it before. *Queer*, you say. *Queer little thing, queer as in opportunist*, you say.

And I think I might smile quietly inside, understanding that for some time, I've been the site of your laundering—oh it's quite simple, how sad. But none of it has worked, because of course it can't. You cannot be reborn fucking me on the living room floor. I established years ago that there was no living room and no floor, to say nothing of the me. The floor and the fucking are gone—so gone.

The camera cuts away, and you slap me so hard, you knock a tooth out of my mouth, but I'm kind of smiling.

45

It's a fact that I'm a problem for you. Now I can see it.

It's just a fact that I'm a threat that cannot be neutralized by possession. By accumulation. Add me to the miles-long list, assign me a number or even a different name or whatever you want, but something will linger: I'm not reducible. None of us is. For some reason, this is a problem for you.

You show your hand the moment you break all the rules you set—the ones you needed to set, because you don't know what love is, and you don't know how to be watchful, don't know how to swim, because you've always been water. You're all the same. All the fucking same. How can you be so big? So fundamental? Why does so much of everything operate according to you?

Affluence without abundance *is* possible, even if you say it's not.

———

The space of the bed or the rug on the living room floor: not much more than a few square feet, but some strange room into which we step, where anything is possible, where nothing else exists. Where for a few moments, you stop counting.

And I stop noticing how you operate, because I am tumbling in the surf of feeling, nothing but feeling feeling, *how does it feel*. And I am very rich. The richest woman in the solar system.

But that is not the whole story. The door can be opened, the rug can be rolled up, the room can disappear, it can just dissolve —I've seen it.

———

You looked at me and said, *No one will ever want to fuck you again*, and I said, *Fine*. You said, *Your heart or whatever it is, it's a wasteland, how do you just love like that, all the way, all the way through? It's impossible*, and I said, *Fine*. Knowing all the while that my heart opens onto a horizon—an endless horizon—whether you see it or not.

I do not see the point, unless we are risking ourselves.

I have stopped feeling hunger. It's gone. You took it from me. You beat it out of me. I beat it out of me. It's gone. Once I saw how stupid it was, how it was just another instance of pleasure built on distant suffering, it disappeared.

You couldn't meet my gaze—still can't. Silently, I said, *So help me god, I will show you yourself*. I know it was probably just as useless as any other prayer, though.

I blinked hard, hoping you'd disappear in the space of the blink, but you didn't. The hunger did, though. It fell away. I wanted to have nothing to do with taking. Thanks to you, I became content to starve. I understood Simone Weil for the first time.

I understood her death.

———

I understand now that I can know something with every cell in me and outside of me and still not know how to act on it or from it, and I understand that this is just called living, most of the time.

I understand that all that matters is whether I can find your eyes and see what I can see in them. Like the way that it doesn't matter whether someone is beautiful or handsome or sexy, because it only matters what kind of desire you can see in their eyes, and whether it's the kind of desire you want or need. It's whether the fact of your energies exchanging would produce anything valuable. It's whether the fact of the exchange would be altering. If only I could find your eyes, your face, your form. But I cannot.

What are those times? you seemed to once ask me, *Those times when your body met another and you could not turn back?* Moments of no return, I understood.

The question is, what will be the content of those moments of no return to come? Will I know they're happening as they're happening? Or will I only be capable of knowing that anything happened in retrospect?

———

I know now that I want you to have an experience with me. Yes, I wanted it all along. I wanted you to steal me. I want to be *the site* of your experience.

Live it through me. Live it in me.

Maybe there was never another way—maybe I just finally understand life. Is this what the mystics knew?

46

Now I know you well enough to know that you don't mean any of it. Each of your girlfriends boyfriends children parents lovers pets ghosts will hate me for all of eternity and even longer, and even that makes me love them. I love them. Is it them you murder each night instead of me?

———

Such a perfect pussy, you tell me, and tell me and tell me. So?

This is it baby, you say. Again and again. Your eyes or whatever closed, closed so tight, squeezed shut, saying, *You're it baby*, you are *it* as you recede and dissolve and reappear. But no. No no.

Call me "baby" again and I will chop your fucking head off. I understand you now, and this means I know that you don't mean anything. There is no meaning. Not from you. Not anymore. Not right now. I'm not angry—please don't get me wrong. I'm just ready.

———

I am carving at my heart, carving at myself. *I* hold the knife—fuck a camera, it's a knife I hold. Not you. I can trust myself with it; I have only myself to cut.

Am I ready to suffer? Yes I am ready to suffer.

Is it strange that it's this painful? I can feel our mutual dissolution. Into each other, I think. Is it dying? I don't know. Maybe this is what freedom feels like.

Is there some *better* way to die?

———

Everything softens in response. Everything goes liquid. Like tears of gratitude.

I am back at the beginning.

47

What remains?

I could never understand why everyone else wanted to fill the void—or why they bothered to try. It seemed like such hubris to me. The best I could hope for was not being consumed by it—being able to exist in relation to it—not being sucked in and taken down and snuffed out by it. Could I let it in? Could I offer it residence here? What other choice did I have?

You are a creature who understands this, whatever you are, and so I fight to keep you close. I see it now. If I don't fight to keep you close, I will die a soul-death. Everything in me needs everything in you. You are not like the rest.

Once, I caught a glimpse of something you had written about me: *I thought "sorry" was the only thing you'd ever say to me.*

I knew the moment you were referring to. We had not yet spoken, and I hadn't noticed you walking behind me in the hall, so that when I let the door close behind me without holding it for you, noticing you just a moment too late, I uttered the word reflexively. I had been surprised to see you there. Your eyes flashed with their characteristic depth. I remember something registering within me: the forces that animate you are not the usual ones. You blaze through life, with grace and patience, somehow. Your eyes gave you away; I was humiliated by what I saw in them.

Lux aeterna in them.

———

You have always refused to call yourself an artist of any sort, though those with sight can see that you're more of an artist than most. Your life is your work of art. You live so well. With more bravery than I can imagine.

What I saw in those words is what I still see: the ability to inhabit yourself so fully that you only need to write one sentence. The clearest vision. Vulnerability that makes no apologies for itself.

You have nothing to prove, and it has always been this way.

———

It's not an unfounded concern, though, that someone like me might not offer anything more than apology. Not everyone has your bravery, you know.

That I can offer more than *sorry* to anyone has so much to do with you. I have learned how to live from you. Like every true artist, you had no idea you were teaching me as you were teaching me. You never thought you *had* anything to teach me. With your life, you tell me, *Do not hold back.*

You are more alive than most. You are more. You've shown me how to live more than I think I can live—how to exceed.

"Art is the consequence of that energy or force that puts life at risk for the sake of intensification, for the sake of sensation itself—not simply for pleasure or for sexuality [...], but for what can be magnified, intensified, for what is more."

For what is more. I believe you are more. I believe you are the thing called art. Our experiment in living is the intensification. This is all there is to art.

You are my favorite artist. Or *non*-artist. *Non-,* because you exceed all existing categories of artistry. You make me an artist. Or non-artist. You see everything in me that I have learned to hide.

You see my love for you, and you do not want to punish me for it. You accept it, and it multiplies. You offer it, give it back, already multiplied, and it continues to multiply. I can trust you with making me, as you can trust me. Is it possible?

———

Once, I watched your eyes as you accepted the inevitability of your own death. It was a tenderness, a softening, a surrender that only the most powerful can achieve. I was drawn and quartered by the beauty I saw there.

I sat on the hospital floor, and I cried. We had not given up— in all those years—we had not stopped trying to understand each other. We had not abandoned the struggle, the tension. We had not stopped trying to see. I was swimming again, but the water was different, or I was different in it. Or, finally I was it, and it was me, and it was a beautiful, perfect hell.

In my dreams, I never fly, but I do breathe underwater.

In the morning, we learned that the test results revealed nothing significant, nothing troubling. The mystery remained unanswered, unexplained, and death would wait for a while longer. We don't get to know how long. The biggest dissolution was yet to come—*is* yet to come.

———

Filling the void was no way to neutralize it, anyhow. Together, we know this. As far as I could tell, the more a person seemed convinced that they'd done it—filled it in—the more asleep at the wheel they seemed to be. Together, we asked: how rich and intense could living be if we attempted the *more*, for what is more. Together we tried. Another great dissolution.

This thing called love, this expansive liquid horizon, it exists for what is more. The normal workings of the world are not in place there, though there is nothing more normal, more banal, more mundane, more earthly.

There is an intimacy that permeates. I'm not quite sure how, but it is there.

48

I felt you taking a very particular form. I felt you approaching as Death herself, and I asked myself: *Should I be afraid?*

There are other questions to ask, too: what is left to lose, when the doctor cocks her head and looks at you, rattled, saying, *The good news is that we might have caught it early?*

What is left to lose when you go from the biopsy to your daughter's school, retrieving her at the end of the day, and she hugs you with her four-year-old intensity and honesty?

What is left to lose when the person in bed with you curls around you, clutching you desperately to him, saying nothing but saying everything with his silent tears?

What is left?

———

I want to be at this intellectual, psychological, emotional fighting weight until the day I go. Will I have this luxury?

Should I just go now? There are many ways to do it. I think about those ways a lot, sometimes more than I can admit to myself. I've already done more living than most, in only 35 years, and I know it. Should I be greedy enough to ask for more?

I have tried to say to myself: *If what you're doing is not essential, just stop it now, if you can.* Am I living essentially?

———

I know what's left.

What's left is the only certainty I can claim: that as I wait for *the results,* I am living some fundamental human motion or movement, an internal dance.

Is today the day? Which day will be the day? What will I have done in the meantime? Has it been worth it?

It's the ability to ask these questions that is left to lose. With ourselves, with each other.

We all want to know how long we'll have to ask them, but *how long* is a secret. A real secret is never told. And there is no one to tell us anyhow.

Not even you can tell me.

———

Then another shift, and you are not Death anymore, you are back to no particular form. And I just don't know. Maybe this new language will fail me, or maybe I will not be capable of doing it justice—maybe *I* will fail *it.*

How long do I have to work at it to find out?

———

Forever, Lindsay. Forever. Are you ready to suffer?

———

I dream of revelations for you and everyone like you. Everyone like me. I have to admit it. No more pretending I don't see myself in you. Your desperation. Your worldlessness.

I know. I know—I really do. It is hard to know what I'm living for. You have never known what you're living for. But you continue. You know why, don't you? Please tell me you do. Tell me you know something the rest of us don't. Tell me it's not just viral replication all the way down.

———

The dark wilderness stalks you. I can see it. I see it in your eyes. Nothing you could do could cover it all the way up. Not the drugs. Not the drinks. Not the brave swagger. Not the hundreds of people you've seduced, bedded, left for dead. Not the look you give me. You don't fool me for a minute. Your heart is soft and malleable, and I can see it in even the way you bring a glass to your lips. Gentle and persistent as the sound of you breathing in deep sleep, you reveal yourself.

———

Our lacerations coincide, but somehow I have been able to climb out from time to time, finding a moment to stitch myself up, to grow a new skin. This fact binds us to each other. But it is a mystery to me—what has made it possible for me to climb out. You ask me, and I keep saying, *I don't know.* Some things float, some things sink.

I drive my hand into the dirt as hard as I can, because it's all I've got. It's the only thing I get to know.

———

The emptiness turns you inside out. The longing, despite and yet also because of the emptiness. Each time you admit the emptiness to me, I see you in my dreams. All of you. You come to me in sleep, the surest sign I have that you've cracked me open with your admissions. I wake each time in the morning, resigned to the longing that will trail me. You don't appreciate the difference between melancholy and despair; I am always at risk of following you there.

I have, quite simply, loved you and wanted you to stay alive. I'm not sure if you've ever known what you've wanted. But I cannot hand off my desires for your life to you. It doesn't work that way. Showing you the depth of my feeling—of my care for you—will not make you capable of anything.

The question, as always, as we all know, is what we will do to make it through. There is a vast buffet of nearly everything, but is any of it what we need?

Can it be right that *making* is the key? Making is the ultimate act of care, so far as I can tell. It's the only thing that has kept me alive, and I know that it's keeping some of you alive—giving care, *being* care.

———

What is the sound of human longing? What does it look like? Does it have a color? Take a particular shape? If you could sculpt it, paint it, draw it, sing it, inhabit it fully in order to give it corporeal weight, would that be enough for you? Would it be sufficient? Would you stand back and brush your hands and say, *Ok, ça suffit?* No. Never. I see you. For you, it couldn't be. You would die or dissolve or disappear even faster if the satisfaction set in. Is it cruel for me to want you to keep living?

Keep your hands off it—that thing you need to make to get by. Let it be. No, wait. Keep at it, please.

Please. For all of us. You'll get there. Won't you?

49

Dear You,

The remnants of longing. Do you dream of me? Do you know that I exist? Do you know that I am sometimes a person? Are you a thing that thinks? I will no longer ask, What are you? because it does not matter. Do you feel ashamed when you think of me? Of all of us? Of everything? Or do you feel pride? Are you proud that I've understood, proud that I can see?

My last night really with you, I lived deeper in hell than I ever had before. It was not the hell of approaching and eating Lispecter's cockroach, though I wondered if it might be. It was the hell of having already eaten it, but not letting myself admit and understand that. It was the hell of not letting myself act on how much I did not need you anymore, not with the cockroach swimming in my belly. You got in me as deep as you could—it went too far. I don't know how, but I know it went too far; I was too close to leaving this form.

That last night, I struggled to breathe and I could feel my heart slowing. I might have been ready to give up, give in. I might have been willing myself to let go. I might have wanted very badly to die. Sometimes you just let go of life. You just let it go.

But no. From somewhere within me, I shouted to myself, shouted so loud: *Survive if you can, then get the fuck out.* Get the fuck out. Even if there is no *out*. Get there.

I watched each of you, each of your insignificant incarnations breathe, I felt each of you curled around me in the night, watched your profile in the partial moonlight, and I thought: how is *that* possible—to just breathe and sleep and *exist*? Go on, tell your friends, tell them all. Tell them you killed me. It's partially true anyhow.

Are you ready to suffer? Are you?

———

You left me for dead, time and time again. But I made it through —I keep making it through—and although I am dying same as everything, I am not dead yet.

I think I left a light on inside me. I cohere here, for this moment, and I accept the responsibility it entails. I see. I cannot say *what*, but I know. See-feel-know. It is a node within a network within a node within a network within a node within a network ad infinitum. I do know you.

———

I wanted to take your breath away, wanted to know I was real, to see it in the constriction and expansion of the rise and fall of your chest. But I was wrong. I didn't need to know this way. I knew already.

You are with me forever, and now I understand it as a gift. As no-gift-is-pure-gift. As infinite terror. As the weight of responsibility, as one site of your expression, as the prerequisite for everything. I am sorry that I sometimes hate you, but there's no other way it could be. We are the same, and the same thing, but also not.

———

We are going somewhere, out there past the horizon, together but not. The only difference: I know that I am alone and dying; I have felt you convincing yourself through me that you are not. I will keep using it to transform, as you keep going (living?), convinced that you are not alone, not dying.

But you are alone, and though you will never die, I still know that you are dying. See you in the next world, baby.

It's never over. One day, I will return to liquid, and I will not be sad.

I know that nothing just expires and then moves on. There are traces everywhere, yes I am ready to suffer. Traces everywhere. Never over.

———

There were finger-shaped bruises on my hips and on my arms, and as I watched them fade, I wanted to paint them on fresh each day, wanted to tattoo them on my flesh, so that I might remember: this is what happens, and this is how it feels. So that I might remember: protect what it is in you that gives love. Protect it, goddammit. Protect it protect it. Protect it fearlessly. That's all.

That's all.

ENDNOTES

PROLOGUE

1. "The Same Situation," *Court and Spark*, 1974.

CHAPTER 2

1. Sylvia Plath, "Daddy."
2. Sara Ahmed, *The Promise of Happiness*.
3. Simone Weil, ibid.

CHAPTER 8

1. Elizabeth Herzog, Margaret Mead, Mark Zborowski, *Life is With People*.
2. Kathy Acker, *Blood and Guts in High School*.

CHAPTER 12

1. Lawrence," *Donkey Gospel*
2. Hélène Cixous, *Three Steps on the Ladder of Writing*.

CHAPTER 14

1. Friedrich Nietzsche, *Thus Spoke Zarathustra*.
2. Lou Andreas Salomé, *The Erotic*.
3. Ibid.
4. *You Alone Are Real To Me, Remembering Rainer Maria Rilke by Lou Andreas-Salomé*, translated by Angela von der Lippe.
5. Lou Andreas Salomé, *The Erotic*.

CHAPTER 17

1. Gunnhild Øyehaug, *Knots*.
2. Nietzsche, posthumous notes, 1881.
3. Jean-François Lyotard, *Why Philosophize?*

CHAPTER 20

1. Hélène Cixous, *Three Steps on the Ladder of Writing*.

CHAPTER 32

1. Orhan Pamuk, *Istanbul*.
2. "*Hüzün*, the Turkish word for melancholy, has an Arabic root; when it appears in the Koran (as *huzn* in two verses and *hazen* in three others) it means much the same thing as the contemporary Turkish word. The Prophet Muhammad referred to the year in which he lost both his wife Hatice and his uncle Ebu Talip, as *Sennetul huzn, the year of melancholy*; this confirms that the word is meant to convey a feeling of deep spiritual loss. But if *hüzün* begins its life as a word for loss and the spiritual agony and grief attending it, my own readings indicate a small philosophical fault line developing over the next few centuries of Islamic history. With time, we see the emergence of two very different *hüzüns*, each evoking a distinct philosophical tradition. According to the first tradition, we experience the thing called *hüzün* when we have invested too much in worldly pleasures and material gain; the implication is, 'If you hadn't involved yourself so deeply in this transitory world, if you were a good and true Muslim, you wouldn't care so much about your worldly losses.' The second tradition, which rises out of Sufi mysticism, offers a more positive and compassionate understanding of the word and of the place of loss and grief in life. To the Sufis, *hüzün* is the spiritual anguish we feel because we cannot be close enough to Allah, because we cannot do enough for Allah in this world. A true Sufi follower would take no interest in worldly concerns like death, let alone goods or possessions; he suffers from grief, emptiness, and inadequacy because he can never be close enough to Allah, because his apprehension of Allah is not deep enough. Moreover, it is the absence, not the presence, of *hüzün* that causes him distress. It is the failure to experience *hüzün* that leads him to feel it; he suffers because he has not suffered enough, and it is by following this logic to its conclusion that Islamic culture has come to hold *hüzün* in high esteem. If *hüzün* has been central to Istanbul culture, poetry, and everyday life over the past two centuries, if it dominates our music, it must be at least partly because we see it as an honor." Ibid.
3. Ibid.
4. Ibid.

CHAPTER 34

1. Catherine Malabou, *Changing Difference*, quoting Luce Irigaray, *Ethics of Sexual Difference*.
2. Georges Bataille, *The Accursed Share*, Vol. 1.

3. Georges Bataille, *Guilty*.
4. Catherine Malabou, *Changing Difference?*.

CHAPTER 40

1. John Dewey, *Art as Experience*.
2. Maurice Blanchot, *The Space of Literature*.

CHAPTER 43

1. Anaïs Nin, *Henry and June*.
2. Anne Dufourmantelle, *Power of Gentleness*.
3. Anaïs Nin, *Henry and June*.
4. Jacques Derrida, *The Gift of Death*.
5. Anaïs Nin, Ibid.
6. Richard Alpert / Ram Dass, *Be Here Now*.

THANK YOU

The author wishes to thank Charlene Elsby, B.R. Yeager, Kathe Koja, Elle Nash, Rebecca van Laer, Lucca Fraser, Kate Reed Petty, Christoph Paul, Leza Cantoral, Suzanne McCullagh, Kelly Jones, Andrew Robinson, Chioke I'Anson, Philippe, and Sabine.

Parts of this book were first published at Forever Magazine, Hobart, Expat, and SELFFUCK. Parts of this book were written at Unruly Retreat in Rice, Virginia, thanks in large part to the generosity of Hayley DeRoche.

ABOUT THE AUTHOR

Lindsay Lerman's first book *I'm From Nowhere* was published in 2019. Her essays, short stories, and poetry have been published in The Los Angeles Review of Books, Entropy, Hobart, Southwest Review, and elsewhere. She is currently adapting her short story *Real Love*—which first appeared in NY Tyrant Magazine—for the screen. She is represented by Abby Walters at CAA.

ALSO BY CLASH BOOKS

CLASH

WE PUT THE LIT IN LITERARY

clashbooks.com

FOLLOW US

Twitter

IG

FB

@clashbooks

EMAIL

clashmediabooks@gmail.com

PUBLICITY

clashbookspublicity@gmail.com